MW01485439

# SILK SUIT/STONE HEART

## THE SECOND CAT LEIGH AND MARCI WELLES CRIME NOVEL

### DONNA M. CARBONE

WRITE FOR YOU, LLC

*Silk Suit/Stone Heart* is a work of fiction. Names, characters, businesses, organizations, events and incidents either are the product of the author's imagination or are used fictitiously. Any references to historical events, real people, living or dead, or real locales are used fictitiously.

Copyright © 2016 by Donna M. Carbone. All rights reserved. No part of this story may be reproduced or retransmitted in any form or by any electronic or mechanical means, including information storage and retrieval systems, without permission in writing from the author, except by a reviewer who may quote brief passages in a review.

For information, contact:
Write For You, LLC
Palm Beach Gardens, Florida 33410
www.writeforyoullc.com

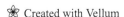 Created with Vellum

# ACKNOWLEDGMENTS

Many thanks to everyone who read the first Cat Leigh and Marci Welles crime novel, *Through Thick and Thin*. Your kind words and support inspired me to keep writing. I want to extend a special note of gratitude to Deborah Weed—a kindred spirit if ever there was one—for continually boosting my self-confidence. I also want to thank my good friend and beta reader extraordinaire, Gale Richards, for her patience and attention to detail. Without her dedication, this book would still be in the planning stages. And big hugs to my good friends John Paul Gasca, Chesta Drake and Candy Cohn, who never fail to mention me on Facebook with encouraging words of praise. Love you, all.

Very special thanks to my son, Michael, who is a brilliant writer and an insightful editor. His suggestions turned a good story into something so much better. Words cannot express my gratitude to my husband, Mike—the wind beneath my wings. He took over all the household chores, including dusting, vacuuming, mopping, shopping and laundry, so I could pursue my passion. I am especially grateful that he turned out to be an excellent cook! Not so happy about the extra pounds that have found their way to my hips, but I just can't resist his special pasta dishes.

A debt of gratitude is owed to my daughter, Jessica Carbone

McKinney, whose photographs always grace the covers of my books and to Kevin Mayle, who works tirelessly to turn those covers into something memorable.

As always, I want to thank both Jessica and the daughter of my heart, Mary Bedwell Bain, for allowing me to use them and their friendship as inspiration for the Cat Leigh and Marci Welles series. You are amazing women... exemplary role models ... who inspire me daily to be better than I ever imagined I could be.

*"Damn girl, you can write!*
*Burt Reynolds*

# PROLOGUE

*A*lthough the New Year was nearly two weeks gone, there remained a lingering sense of holiday cheer in the air. Wire candy canes covered in red and white plastic fringe still hung from street lights along PGA Boulevard in Palm Beach Gardens, while store windows festooned with green and gold garland announced a *LAST CHANCE* to buy after Christmas bargains.

For Homicide Detectives Jessica "Cat" Leigh and Marcassy "Marci" Welles, this seasonally chilly Saturday evening was definitely a reason to celebrate. It was the partners first night off in nearly four months. They were exhausted from carrying a heavy case load and had been eagerly anticipating an evening out since the clocks had jumped ahead an hour the previous November. Quiet dinners in restaurants that did not require plastic utensils and styrofoam takeout containers were special occasions that usually happened only when the dusting of white powder on city streets was actual snow. Since the likelihood of that happening in south Florida was never, getting through an evening on the town without a call from the Palm Beach County Sheriffs' Office dispatcher was a miracle. Thus, it was with great surprise that Cat, Marci and their significant others found themselves seated in a secluded corner of the River House Restaurant in the Soverel Harbour Marina at 7:30 pm on Saturday, the 13th of January.

Cat, long blonde hair cascading to near her waist, was dressed in her usual fashionista style while Marci had exchanged her uniform—heavy rubber soled shoes and man tailored slacks and jacket—for stilettos and a Jones of New York black a-line dress bought on sale at TJ Maxx. The high heels were a necessity as, when not carrying a gun on her hips, her petite stature usually caused her to be overlooked in a crowd. Her short, dark hair encased her freckle-sprinkled face like fili-gree framing a cameo and, when seen in profile, her alabaster skin completed the illusion. More accustomed to being seen as zaftig rather than a sex symbol, she could not resist twirling around like a plastic ballerina atop a little girl's jewelry box as her dinner companions showered her with praise.

So startling was Marci's transformation from tough cop to wicked woman that Cat, her fiancé Kevin and Marci's husband Ian, spent most of the meal toasting her new look. By the time they finished their steak and shrimp dinners, there were two empty bottles of Brunello di Montalcino on the table attesting to the expensive sincerity of their compliments.

"I've been trying to get you into a dress for years," Cat smiled her approval at her long-time best friend. "The last time I saw you in heels was senior prom. You didn't even wear heels for your wedding. You look amazing, Marci."

The two couples were practically giddy both from having imbibed a fair amount of fermented grapes and at having an uninterrupted couples' night which did not require a diaper bag, squeaky toys and cheerios. Sonora Leslie, Marci's and Ian's 22- month-old daughter, was having a night out of her own—a sleepover at Grandma Nancy's house. So heady was the feeling of freedom that the couples decided to order dessert, coffee and after dinner drinks. That was their first mistake.

As they sipped their Sambuca-laced espressos, the conversation veered to a case Marci and Cat had recently investigated—a road rage incident that had turned into murder by Louisville Slugger. Since the suspect was in custody and the local newspapers had his face and name plastered all over their front pages, the partners felt comfortable discussing the details of the crime. As some of the more gruesome aspects were revealed, they remained oblivious to the less than thrilled looks being cast their way by Ian and Kevin.

According to Amarus Sanchez, the wife of the late Domingo Sanchez, she had sat petrified in the front passenger seat of the family's Dodge Ram pickup while Ricardo Ruiz stood on the hood of the truck and smashed the windshield. She had watched horrified, screaming until her voice was nothing more than a rasp, as her husband's upper torso was pulled through the broken window and his head bashed in. The sound of her terrified screams made their attacker laugh more manically with each swing of the bat.

Ruiz was no stranger to law enforcement in Florida. His rap sheet included being sentenced to seven years for firing 10 rounds at a Riviera Beach family during a holiday gathering in 2003. Jevon Wilson, the owner of the home where the shooting took place, told police that he had argued with Ruiz earlier in the day but, since they had settled their differences, he gave the altercation no further thought. Once the shooting began, it became obvious that Ruiz, who was a member of the Spanish Cobras gang, did not share Wilson's "It's over. Let's forget about it" mindset.

As the sun stroked the horizon, Ruiz drove slowly past the house on Jog Road where Wilson's mother, wife and infant daughter were sitting on the front porch and opened fire. Whether intentional or not, the three family members were unharmed by the spray of bullets. Only a few cars were hit and the living room window shattered. Ruiz was quickly arrested but, since the only damage was to property, when found guilty of first degree assault and carrying a pistol without a permit, his sentence was reduced to three years. He served his time without incidence. No sooner was he back on the streets than he was back in trouble.

Domingo Sanchez was not as lucky as the three Wilson females. The detailed report given by his wife stated that the incident began when her husband cut Ruiz off while driving south on the I-95. "We had to get in front of him. He was veering from left to right, crossing into one lane and then the other. We were afraid to get caught behind him or to even be near him. Our exit was coming up, and we just wanted to get off the highway."

Mr. and Mrs. Sanchez lived in Delray Beach and, as they approached the Atlantic Avenue exit ramp, Ruiz caught up to them, honking his horn and giving them the finger. He drove threateningly close to the Sanchez's truck and threw a handful of change at the vehicle. Some of the coins sailed through the open window, hitting Domingo Sanchez in the eye.

Concerned that his sight had been impaired, Sanchez pulled over on the exit ramp. Ruiz also pulled over and, baseball bat in hand, walked back toward the pickup. Words flew and when it became obvious that Ruiz was out of control, Amarus Sanchez pleaded with her husband to get back in the truck, which he did. The next thing they knew, Ruiz was standing on the hood and swinging at the windshield with all his might. He did not stop until what was left of Mr. Sanchez's head hung from his neck like a smashed pumpkin, blood and brains covering both the hood and the inside of the vehicle as well as Mrs. Sanchez's face and clothing.

"Truthfully," Ian Welles said to his wife, "this is not how I had hoped to end our evening. It doesn't seem to matter how long we are married or how often I read and hear about these crimes, they never get less disturbing. It's hard for me to believe that you and Cat can see such violence and not be affected by it, especially after those lunatics ruined the holidays for so many families in Palm Beach County. I don't think I will ever forget the horrible way those people died."

"I doubt any of us will ever forget Harold Kruge, Mace Maloney and Auric Anderson. The Kalendar Killers have left their mark are far too many lives," Marci agreed with her husband.

The Kalendar Killer case involved a series of five brutal murders over an eight month period. Each of the murders took place on a major holiday and each of the victims was found in a public place wrapped in a banner proclaiming "Happy" whatever special day was being observed. Solving the crimes had put Cat and Marci in the spotlight for nearly a year. Mother's Day, Father's Day, Independence Day, Labor Day, Halloween and Thanksgiving would never again be celebrated without members of the Palm Beach County Sheriff's Office Violent Crimes Division and their families offering a moment a silence for the victims.

During the early stages of the investigation, local media had described Cat and Marci as inept and then, after they had solved what had at first appeared to be an unsolvable mystery, as heroes. Neither title appealed to the detectives. Their job was to protect and serve. Nothing else mattered. Friends, family and co-workers knew that the one character trait they were most proud of was one they did not have... ego.

To make matters worse, an independent film company with a very low budget and even lower ethics made an unauthorized movie entitled *The Kalendar Killers* in which inexperienced actors portrayed not only Cat and Marci but also the victims. The producers and director did not bother with the facts of the case but, rather, sensationalized the murders by focusing on the slasher aspects.

"Sweetie," Marci commiserated with Ian, "I'm sorry talking about this case has upset you. For Cat and me... well, we've just gotten used to it. It isn't that we aren't bothered by the crimes. It's that we're no longer surprised by the brutality people inflict upon one another."

"I know and I admire the lengths to which the two of you go to keep this community safe, but let's talk about something else. Cat, I must compliment you on choosing this restaurant. The food was all you promised it would be."

"Thanks, Ian."

Cat squeezed Kevin's knee under the table as a silent apology should he, too, be disturbed by the conversation. "The River House has been a favorite of mine for a long time, not just because seeing the waiters make Caesar salad the old-fashioned way reminds me of Easter Sunday dinners at my grandmother's restaurant in New Jersey. As a little girl, I loved 'the show' as I used to call it."

"I didn't know your grandmother owned a restaurant." Ian looked at Marci as if to ask why she had never told him such an interesting detail about Cat's life.

"La Vecchia Lanterna. I can't believe Marci never told you. I know I've mentioned my Uncle Ducky numerous times."

"You have. I remember thinking that was a weird name for a grown man. Don't know why I never told Ian about him." Marci shrugged her shoulders. "How did your uncle get that name?"

"Uncle Ducky was really Uncle Donald. Seems he was a slow talker when he was a toddler. No amount of encouragement could get him to say Mama or Dada or baba... nothing. He was mute. By the time he was three, my grandparents were worried and frustrated. One day, they took Uncle Donald to the zoo and, as soon as he saw the ducks, he began to quack. From that moment on, he was Ducky."

"I'm assuming he did eventually speak."

"Of course. Actually started that very day. Full sentences and complex thoughts. You couldn't shut him up. Turned out he was gifted."

"And he ran the restaurant?"

"Let's just say he had his finger in a lot of enterprises, not all of them successful or legal. He was, however, a great chef and made a to-die-for Caesar salad dressing."

Kevin and Ian hated just about every ingredient in a Caesar salad, including the Romaine lettuce. Neither they nor Marci shared Cat's palate-pleasing enthusiasm for the recipe or the presentation. "If you could deep fry the green stuff, I'm sure I'd change my mind," Kevin usually replied whenever Cat mentioned healthy eating. Both he and Ian had a penchant for anything that could be plunged into boiling oil although they did draw the line at the cheeseburgers topped with a scoop of deep-fried cinnamon ice cream often served at the South Florida Fair.

Whereas Cat enjoyed watching as the over-sized wooden bowls were rubbed with garlic cloves before being mashed with salt and anchovies, Marci preferred slathering her iceberg with ranch dressing. While Cat savored the sight of the raw eggs being whisked with lemon juice, mustard, olive oil and Parmesan cheese, Marci held her napkin to her face and pretended to gag. To Cat, a few extra anchovies and fresh ground pepper were the perfect finishing touches. To Marci, croutons added just the right crunch. The one thing they did agree on was that wine made everything taste better.

After dinner drinks and dessert had just been delivered to their table when a familiar face entered the restaurant. Jon Everett Gardner had been the governor of Florida from 1971 to 1979. With him were his wife, Eileen, and his Secretary of State, Alvin Langdon, and his wife, Tracy.

Gardner was a career politician who, despite the passage of more than three quarters of a century of birthdays, had an encyclopedic memory for names and faces. Although it had been 40 years since he called the Governor's Mansion in Tallahassee home, he never missed an opportunity to shake a hand or pat someone on the back.

Upon entering the River House's main dining room, Governor Gardner had immediately recognized Cat and Marci, who were something of minor celebrities since solving the Kalendar Killer murders. Before settling down to peruse the menu, he stopped to express his appreciation to his "… two favorite detectives" for their service to Palm Beach County and the State of Florida.

The cordialities over, Cat, Marci, Ian and Kevin turned their attention back to talk of personal matters and paid no more attention to the Gardeners and Langdons other than to say that he was "… always a gentleman." Occasionally, when a burst of loud laughter pierced the air, Cat and Marci would look over and smile in appreciation of what was, obviously, a good time. The Governor had mentioned that he and "the Mrs." were celebrating 60 years of happy marriage. From the way Eileen Gardener hung on her husband's words and the way she affectionately stroked his arm, it was impossible to miss that the love light in her eyes was still shining brightly.

Cat had just licked the last bit of cannoli cream from her dessert fork when the scream from a nearby table brought the evening to a sudden halt. Eileen Gardener stood with her hands to her mouth staring down at her husband's body, which lay crumbled on the floor. Keeping Mrs. Gardner from collapsing in a faint was Alvin Langdon.

Although Cat and Marci had not been watching what was happening at the Governor's table closely, to their trained eyes it appeared that no sooner had the Governor swallowed his first forkful of salad than the frivolity turned to terror. Hysteria replaced happiness as he toppled to the floor, a foamy sputum forming on his lips.

Marci and Cat immediately rose and rushed to help. That was their second mistake of the night. Had they stayed in their seats, what followed would have become the responsibility of responding officers called to the scene by the house manager. However, Marci and Cat lived their lives by upholding their oath of service. They had pledged to put the public's needs before their private wants and desires and helping a former governor was a top priority. The effects of the wine dissipated in the few seconds it took them to get to their feet.

Marci got down on her knees to check for a pulse while Cat held out her badge and identified herself to the manager, who stood averting his eyes from the Governor's body. His legs were shaking so hard and fast that he resembled a dog with fleas. Barely could he string three words together to make a sentence. "He… dead… Is?"

Cat kept her voice low so as not to upset nearby patrons. "I don't know yet. We'll need to secure this area. Please have your staff block all exits to prevent anyone from leaving. That includes your waiters and the kitchen help."

As the manager hurried away to call paramedics, Cat turned to the horrified diners. Most were gaping at the Governor's lifeless body as though expecting to see a reenactment of Lazarus rising from the dead.

"Ladies and gentlemen…" Cat kicked off her shoes and stood atop a chair to address the crowd. "The waiters will escort you to the lounge area. We know you have concerns. You are not in any danger. However, until we know what has happened here, you must remain in the restaurant while police officers take your statements. Please go quietly. Do not remove anything from your table except your personal belongings."

As the patrons filed out of the dining room, Marci continued to perform cardiopulmonary resuscitation techniques. Each time she raised her head to begin chest compressions, she motioned to Cat that the Governor was beyond saving. Cat turned and spoke to Mrs. Gardner and the Langdons.

"Mrs. Gardener, I'm Detective Cat Leigh and the person doing CPR on your husband is my partner, Detective Marci Welles. She will continue applying life-saving measures until emergency medical personnel arrive and take over. I assure you the Sheriff's Office will do everything it can to find out what happened here."

Eileen Gardener grabbed Marci's hand as she spoke. "Thank you, Detective. My husband... is he..." Sobs replaced words as she sank into a chair supported by her friends.

Just then a loud banging was heard on the front door. Cat glanced in the direction of the lobby and saw that the EMTs had arrived. Right behind them was the Violent Crimes Division's superior officer—the deeply gravel-voiced Captain Karen Constantine—motioning frantically to be let in. The Captain had a look of dark anger on her face as she pleaded with a waiter who was taking his job of sentinel a bit too seriously. Despite Captain

Constantine repeatedly stating her name and rank in an ever increasing decibel, the waiter, who opened the door just enough to let the paramedics in, insisted on more identification than the gold shield the Captain held pressed against the glass panel in the door.

Tall, imposing, often sullen, and sporting a scalp-baring Marine regulation haircut, Karen Constantine had eyes the color of charcoal briquettes after a long day of barbecuing. Her unwavering dedication to upholding the law began before birth. Her father, a beat cop in the days when cops actually walked a beat, had had a miniature police uniform specially made for her to wear on the day she was brought home from the hospital.

The Captain wore her badge and gun with a degree of poise few top models possessed when sashaying down a runway. Recently appointed to head up the PBC Sheriff's Office murder and mayhem division, she was making many much needed, but not necessarily liked, changes. Those changes accounted for her nickname, Constantine the Hungarian, a not so flattering reference to the popular sword and sorcery comic book character, Conan the Barbarian.

Marci and Cat admired the Captain and, after being the two lone women in the homicide division for the past few years, were happy to have a superior who understood how hard it was to make it in a man's world. Since Captain Constantine had taken over, Marci and Cat rarely heard their macho-challenged counterparts whisper aspersions about women best serving the department on their backs or knees. So determined was Captain Constantine to avoid sexual harassment charges that she had verbally castrated a male officer her first day on the job after hearing him reference Cat's and Marci's physical appearance by calling them "Thick" and "Thin."

Constantine ruled her little corner of the world with an iron fist. Her voice was nothing if not authoritative. When she spoke, she sounded like a four-pack-a-day smoker although she had never taken so much as a puff in her life. Health conscience, the frown lines on her forehead deepened each time one of her subordinates entered the office followed by a low hanging cloud of nicotine. She cared deeply about the men and women in her charge but she'd be damned before she would allow herself to be seen as a softy. No one was fooled.

Finally having convinced the waiter that she was, indeed, the law, Captain Constantine strode across the dining room with long steps reminiscent of a cheetah stalking its prey. "What happened?" Her strident voice demanded answers from her two top detectives. "How did you get here so fast?"

"We were already here having dinner… sitting just two tables away." Marci hung her shield around her neck as she spoke. "We've put a call in for G. I'm no expert, but I'm certain he will confirm that the Governor was poisoned."

The Captain stared from the paramedics still working over Governor Gardner's body to Marci, a quizzical look in her eyes. "I don't think I've ever seen you in a dress before, Detective."

"And you probably never will again. Nothing good ever comes from trying to be what you're not."

"I see it as just the opposite. Thanks to your evening out, you and Cat were on scene when this crime was committed. That means there's less chance of evidence being removed or tainted. I'd say fashion and fate played equal roles here tonight."

Before Marci could respond, another ruckus at the door announced the arrival of Palm Beach County Medical Examiner Dr. Mark Geschwer, affectionately called "G" by everyone in the Sheriff's Department. The sight of his tuxedo clad torso, so different from his usual outrageously colorful attire, halted further conversation between the Captain, Cat and Marci. His greeting, usually delivered in a hypo-nasal voice reminiscent of Jerry Lewis in the 1963 film *The Nutty Professor*, was subdued.

"Captain. Detectives." A quick nod of his head, and he turned his attention to the EMTs and the late Governor. The law enforcement officers watched as G did his own examination of the body and confirmed what Marci had already stated. Governor Gardner was dead, and it appeared that poisoning was the reason.

"Captain," G requested, "please get a forensics team here asap. We cannot remove the Governor's body until we have collected evidence. Also, please send officers into the kitchen to secure that area. No one is to leave and nothing is to be removed from the cooking surfaces."

G turned to one of the wait staff who was standing nearby. "Get me a table cloth. Let's show the Governor and his wife a little respect by covering his body."

"G, we almost didn't recognize you. Formal attire for a crime scene? Don't tell us… Fred Astaire is your new favorite movie star?" Cat's eyes twinkled as she teased her colleague.

"Not quite, Detective." G spoke in his normal voice which was a soft, soothing mix of southern charm and perfect elocution. "My nephew—my late brother's youngest son—was married today. He honored me by asking that I serve as his best man."

"That's wonderful. So, why are you here? You should be celebrating at the wedding reception."

"I've practically raised this young man since my brother passed. We've shared many moments worthy of celebration and, I believe, there will be many more, but when I heard that Governor Gardner had died… This is where I need to be."

"Well, G, I'm glad you chose to join us." The Captain nodded toward Mrs. Gardner, who was still seated nearby staring at her husband's body. "This is going to be a delicate matter, and there's no one better than you to handle priority post mortems."

"I'll give you a preliminary report in a few minutes. From what I can see, I do believe the Governor was poisoned. The autopsy will have my full attention first thing in the morning."

Once the crime scene was secured, the Governor's body removed and all the witness statements taken, Cat and Marci joined Ian and Kevin in the car for the short drive home. Everyone was tired, but Cat was chatty… the evening's crime having resurrected the memory of a similar event her parents had experienced years earlier.

"Did I ever tell you about the time my parents were out to dinner and a man died at the next table?"

A chorus of "No's" answered from the car's dark interior and, with encouragement from three now wide awake people, Cat told her story.

"In the town where my family lived before moving to Palm Beach County, there was a lovely seafood restaurant called Harbor Lights. The food was outstanding, and the ambiance was just the right blend of formal and casual. Not stuffy but definitely not a jeans and tee shirt kind of place.

Saturday nights usually found my parents at *their* table. So often did they eat at Harbor Lights that they had taken to thinking of the secluded booth overlooking the gardens as their own. On this particular evening, they were enjoying a meal of Chateaubriand."

"Okay. I don't want to appear dumb," Ian said, "but what is Chateau whatever you called it?"

Cat laughed. "It's not a popular dish on menus anymore but back then, ordering Chateaubriand was considered very romantic. Think of a piece of filet mignon the size of a small roast beef and decorated with cooked vegetables. It was customary for the meat to be carved table side with dramatic flair.

My parents were watching the waiter perform his magic when two elderly couples were given the table closest to them. My parents smiled; the new arrivals offered a pleasant 'Good Evening' before settling down to peruse the menus. Mom and Dad continued sipping wine and talking, almost totally lost in a world of their own.

Every now and then, my parents would look around the room just to see what was happening and, in so doing, they noticed the progress of those four people. On some level, they were aware that courses were being delivered and that the couples were enjoying themselves. When they told us this story later in the evening, they said that during the early portion of the meal, the foursome seemed to be having a lively discussion, laughing and poking each other for emphasis. That all changed when their main courses were delivered to the table.

One of the gentlemen appeared to have fallen asleep in his chair. His head was tilted forward onto his chest and the position of his body made it difficult for the waiter to place his plate in front of him. Mom and Dad overheard the waiter asking if everything was all right. 'Oh, yes,' the wife responded. 'He often does this. Not to worry.'"

"Wait a minute." Ian once again had questions. "You mean the wife just left him fallen over onto the table?"

"Yup. The waiter left the man's dinner and went off to see to his other customers. My dad, who had been watching for a few minutes, rose and approached the couples' table. He apologized for interrupting but said that he believed the man was in distress. He suggested they call for paramedics.

The wife assured my dad that her husband was fine. She said, 'He does this all the time.' Just as my father was about to walk away, the man's upper body fell forward onto the table. His face nearly landed in his dinner plate. No one seemed to care. The wife stood up and repositioned him in his seat so that he was sitting up straight. Then, she sat down and continued eating and talking with her friends.

My father was certain that everything was not fine. He knew there was a problem, but he was uncomfortable pressing total strangers to do his bidding. He motioned for the manager, who my parents knew personally, and explained his dilemma.

'I think that guy is dead,' my dad told the manager. 'You need to get him out of the restaurant before your patrons panic.'

The manager spoke with the wife, who gave consent to lift her husband's body while still seated in the chair and remove him from the table. The waiters assigned to this less than pleasant task earned an extra tip that night which my mom and dad graciously gave them. Paramedics were called, and the man was whisked away to the hospital. The wife and her friends continued to eat.

When they were through with their dinner and had paid their bill, the wife thanked my parents by saying, 'There was no reason to waste the food. My husband would want us to finish our meals.'

And, with that, they left.

Now, here's the best part. The man had died, but the paramedics revived him in the ambulance. Three weeks later, guess who was seated at that same table while mom and dad were having dinner. Thankfully, my parents were already on dessert when the couples arrived."

"Well," Marci brought the conversation back to the present, "I sincerely doubt we're going to see the Governor at the River House in three weeks."

# CHAPTER ONE

*W*eeks had passed since the death of Jon Everett Gardner and the only clearly definitive piece of information uncovered was that his passing was the result of ingesting a moderate dose of the chemical element polonium-210. The autopsy conducted by G revealed that the Caesar salad eaten by the former Florida governor had been contaminated with the poison. Unfortunately, how it got into the salad was still an unanswered question.

The one possible clue was a mention by several members of the wait staff at the River House of a server who "… looked familiar" but whose name was unknown. Everyone who was scheduled to work the night of the murder was accounted for. Each had given a statement to the officers from the PBSO. No stone had been left unturned in securing the crime scene and, yet, it appeared that a mystery man had moved amid the tables during the height of the dinner hour whom no one could identify.

A few diners mentioned seeing a server rush from the restaurant moments before Governor Gardner fell to the floor but, as he was dressed appropriately, they just thought he was on a break and needed a nicotine fix. By the time Cat and Marci were told of this possible lead, hours had passed, and there was no immediate way to trace his identity.

The only distinctive characteristic he bore was "… curly hair that stood up wildly on his head."

With the help of management, the detectives spent three days perusing hundreds of current and past employee records. Job applications were scrutinized, references were checked for negative comments and duration of employment/reasons for leaving were reviewed. Since turnover in the high stress/low pay restaurant industry is over 60%, there was no one currently on staff who could positively put a name to the face of the curly- haired stranger.

Using the unruly locks as a starting point, Cat and Marci pulled two names from the employment records. One was Bernard McMasters, an Albert Einstein look-alike if ever there was one. The other was Brandon Hanson, a rather cherubic man who appeared to be about 25 but, based on his birth date, was 41.

McMasters was quickly discovered living in Colorado. He had moved to Denver eight years earlier and, when not waiting tables at Beaver Creek Ski Resort, he lived a very different kind of Rocky Mountain high than the one John Denver had sung about. The only negative comment expressed by the catering manager at Beaver Creek was that McMasters' uniform always had a "… cloyingly sweet odor about it." Since weed had been legalized in Colorado, the smell of burned tea leaves often overpowered the sweet vanilla and butterscotch scents of the Ponderosa pines that dotted the landscape.

Brandon Hanson was not so easy to find… at least, not in the physical sense. A search of social media uncovered a man who never finished anything he set out to do. There was an arm's length list of unfulfilled hopes and dreams which he jokingly called his "Wished List." His Facebook page read like a perpetual travelogue with trips that took him from Florida to California to Las Vegas to Philadelphia and back to Florida. He seemed to work just long enough to amass the money needed to get from one place to another.

Despite the somewhat bewildered smile he wore in most of his photos, Brandon's posts showed him to be a gentle soul who sincerely cared about the well being of his fellow man. He worried that all the negativity in the world, in particular, negative advertising, was destroying social equilibrium.

While skimming through Brandon's daily posts, Marci happened upon contact information for his parents. More specifically, she found his mother's name – Dr. Muriel Hanson. Dr. Hanson was a psychiatrist. A quick Google search provided an address and phone number.

Marci also found a comment buried among Brandon's daily, mostly rambling, posts, which referenced a bomb threat at Florida Atlantic University. She mentioned it to Cat, and the detectives decided a trip to the FAU Campus in Jupiter could be enlightening.

First things first, Marci called Dr. Hanson's number and explained to the receptionist the who and why of her call. She was asked to wait and five minutes later, Dr. Hanson came on the line. Courtesies exchanged, Marci requested a time when she and Cat could with meet with her.

At first, the doctor was open to meeting with the detectives, but when Marci mentioned FAU, she became hesitant. Dr. Hanson assured Marci that the only mishap in Brandon's life had taken place in a car wash when he was 17 and newly licensed.

According to his mother, Brandon had not known that the red light at the entrance to the chamber meant STOP. He drove through while another car was still in the tunnel, tearing off his side view mirrors and damaging the rotating arms of the cloth friction wash system.

Although Brandon did crush the trunk of the car in front of him, there was no personal injury so no charges were filed. Mr. and Dr. Hanson paid for the repairs to the other driver's vehicle, the repairs to the motorized shaft that moved the washing strips around a car, and the overtime required for employees to clean up the hundreds of slivers of broken glass from in and around the conveyor track.

Once Marci convinced Dr. Hanson that all present and past employees of the River House were being questioned (a small lie but one for which forgiveness would be granted under the circumstances), she relaxed. Dr. Hanson advised Marci that her son was "… a good boy" and that he had been in Philadelphia retracing his childhood at the time of Governor

Gardner's death. With confirmation that Brandon Hanson had not been in Florida when Governor Gardner was murdered, the meeting was scheduled for a week hence. Brandon was due to return the following Friday.

Everywhere Cat and Marci turned, they hit a dead end. The only thing they knew for sure was how Governor Gardner had died.

"Polonium...," G advised Cat and Marci, "... is not unheard of in the food chain. It is found incrementally in seafood and tobacco. When puffing on a cigarette, a smoker deposits a small amount into his or her airways, delivering radiation directly into surrounding cells."

Since Governor Gardner had never smoked, not even as a rebellious teenager, the tobacco connection could not be made. He was also allergic to seafood so that avenue of investigation was closed as well.

In giving his verbal report to Cat and Marci, G quoted statistics that claimed the lungs of smokers were exposed to four times more polonium than non-smokers and that studies had shown that a person smoking one and a half packs a day could receive radiation in amounts equal to having 300 chest X-rays a year. Like Governor Gardner, Cat and Marci were not smokers so G's lecture, while sufficiently scary, was unnecessary. Knowing that his intentions were meant to enlighten not chastise, the detectives smiled their understanding.

G also explained that polonium was used at textile mills in the production of paper rolls and sheet plastics. Those facts were not relevant either as Governor Gardner had been an attorney before retiring and the closest he now got to paper and plastic was reading the Palm Beach Post every day and drinking bottled water.

Despite the lack of any real evidence that a murder had been committed, Cat and Marci spent a lot of time researching polonium-210. It wasn't every day that they got a case involving a chemical element that had been used to assassinate a Russian Federal Security Bureau agent. Alexander Litvinenko had been an officer in the Russian secret service. According to CIA reports, his specialty was investigating organized crime.

In late 1998, Litvinenko and several other FSB officers accused their superiors of assassinating Russian tycoon and highly influential politician Boris Berezovsky. Litvinenko was arrested on charges of overstepping his authority. He was acquitted; re-arrested and, eventually, acquitted again. With the charges against him dropped, he fled with his family to London where he was granted political asylum. Litvinenko went on to work as a journalist, writer and consultant for British intelligence services. In his writings, he accused the Russian secret service of committing horrendous acts of terrorism in their effort to bring former KGB Lieutenant Colonel Vladimir Putin to power.

In November 2006, Litvinenko fell ill quite suddenly and was hospitalized. After 22 torturous days, he died of what was described as poisoning by radioactive polonium-210. He is listed as being the first known victim of lethal Polonium 210-induced acute radiation syndrome.

Cat and Marci's research also revealed that United Kingdom polonium expert Professor Nick Priest, who at one time had worked at some of Russia's nuclear research facilities, believed that the choice of polonium as a murder weapon in Litvinenko's death was a "... stroke of genius". He was quoted as having said, "... the choice of poison was genius in that polonium, carried in a vial in water, can be carried in a pocket through airport screening devices without setting off any alarms." He also said that, "... once administered, polonium creates symptoms that don't suggest poison for days, allowing time for the perpetrator to make a getaway."

Experts estimated that Litvinenko lingered for almost a month because he ingested less than one millionth of a gram of polonium. A higher dose would have killed him quicker much as it had Governor Gardner.

"Okay. Where does someone... anyone... get their hands on enough polonium to kill in a matter of minutes?" Cat was intrigued and frustrated.

"Not only get their hands on it." Marci said, "They need to know how to use it so that they don't kill themselves. Whoever did this was no novice around radioactive substances. Can you imagine if I had given the Governor mouth to mouth? I'd be laying on a slab in G's autopsy room."

The truth in Marci's words gave both detectives pause to think. In the future, they would need to be more careful before administering to a citizen in need. Terrorists, assassins and just plain, old, ordinary, everyday killers were getting more sophisticated in their methods of committing murder.

The first thing Marci did when arriving at the precinct each morning was to pull the metal file basket that sat at the upper left hand corner of her desk to the center of her blotter. That basket held the open unsolved cases that she and Cat were working on. The two top folders were the most important – Governor Gardner's murder and the still unrecovered bodies of the Ribbon Rapist's last two victims. Marci's routine was to stare at those folders for a few minutes while rubbing her hands together. She always hoped that the static electricity generated would somehow spark an idea that would enable her and Cat to move those files to the right side of the desk where closed cases were stacked, waiting for disposition through the legal system.

Since Governor Gardner's death was considered a high profile murder, the media was clamoring for information. When it was revealed that polonium was the weapon of choice, television, radio and hard copy journalists went crazy both for the uniqueness of the story and with fear that they, too, could fall victim. The public wanted to know if eating out would require ordering head stone with their appetizers.

Due to all the bad press, the tourist trade in south Florida was heading into the brink. Restaurants, with the exception of fast food joints which for some reason people saw as harmless, were closed. Lifeguard stations were shuttered, and the beaches were empty as more and more vacationers spent their money in other states. As if the loss of tourist dollars wasn't enough, the airlines were threatening to cut back on flights to PBIA, Fort Lauderdale and Miami International Airports.

Adding insult to injury, a South Miami police detective was arrested on charges that he had engaged in sexual contact with young girls he oversaw through his work as a mentor with the youth police program. The Florida Department of Law Enforcement has received complaints that the officer had served alcohol to the female cadets in the program before forcing them to have intercourse. Coupled with numerous use of force complaints that had become the standard for anyone arrested in a scuffle with police, all law enforcement personnel, regardless of the agency they represented, were feeling the pressure of unwarranted and undeserved negative publicity.

With the nightly news hurling a barrage of criticism at a small percentage of bad cops while failing to recognize the thousands of police officers who unselfishly put their lives on the line every day to protect their communities, police officers throughout the country were taking a walking on eggshells approach to crime. Homicide Detectives Cat Leigh and Marci Welles were all too familiar with negative publicity having received many a verbal slap in the face from the media during the Kalendar Killer investigation in 2006. They and their colleagues on the force had been preparing for an onslaught of disparaging press ever since Palm Beach County Sheriff Mike Brickshaw had gone on record saying he would support and defend his officers unless and until someone brought him proof of wrongdoing. Unfortunately, his stance only infuriated the minority communities whose members were often deliberate targets for racist cops. Brickshaw's assertions that there were "… good and bad people in every walk of life—doctors, lawyers, accountants, bankers, bakers, butchers… all people," did little to assuage the outrage that was manufactured by paid professional agitators in lower income neighborhoods.

Having a long lineage of law enforcement professionals on her family tree, Cat took the slings and arrows personally. Her paternal grandfather had been a hard core investigator in one of the toughest cities in the country—Camden, New Jersey—at a time when organized crime ran the unions. For more than 25 years, her father had been a police physician in the northern New Jersey town of Fort Lee—gateway to Manhattan via the George Washington Bridge. Forty percent of her father's patients were in law enforcement. Another 40% were the criminals those police officers chased. The remaining 20% were just average folks. Almost all were of Italian descent.

Day after day, week after week, these men sat in her father's waiting room. Some of them were friendly. Some were not. Some were funny. Others were best left alone. Tall, short, fat, skinny, tattooed and toupéed, each was unique in his own way, but the one thing they had in common was a deep dislike for honest labor and an intuitive sense of who to trust. God forbid you gave them reason to distrust you.

Cat had spent her teen years earning her way by running her father's home office. She got to know all the patients well... the good, the bad, the innocent, the guilty and the chameleons, of whom there were many.

Although raised as a pure blooded Italian under the watchful eye of Nonna Zocchio, her maternal great grandmother, Cat's ancestry was more like the League of Nations. Her family tree included traces of Irish, German, English and Scottish. Nonna Zocchio was the matriarch of the family. She had been born in the northern capital of Trento, an Alpine city at the foot of the Dolomite Mountains, and immigrated to America as a young woman. Trento was the educational, scientific, financial and political center for the region. Her paternal great grand-parents came from Rodi Garganico in southeastern Italy. Situated on the Adriatic Sea, Rodi was one of the most popular seaside resorts.

Valuing her Italian heritage as highly as she did, Cat was partial to men with dark hair and eyes. She was not repulsed by someone with a Caesar-esque nose provided the nose didn't enter a room before its owner. When she became engaged to the very blond, very Irish Kevin Kavanagh, the person most surprised was Cat herself. Marci swore that there was a gravitational pull which compelled Cat to hire only Italian doctors and Italian contractors. Her preference for Italian restaurants needed no explanation.

"Italians, like every ethnicity, feel more comfortable among their own kind," Cat said whenever Marci commented on the high percentage of burly Italians with unusual occupational titles Cat had met as a teen. There was The Hammer, Nick the Knuckle, and the less fear-inducing in name only, Red Ritchie—Cat's first crush. Unlike the swarthy men who frequented La Vecchia Lanterna and her father's medical office, Ritchie was a carrot top, tall and thin with startling blue eyes in a handsome and, surprisingly, angelic looking face. Unfortunately, any further association with angels happened only in the hereafter.

Marci loved hearing Cat talk about her youth in New Jersey especially since growing up in West Virginia had been boring by comparison. Whereas Cat's family included some very edgy characters, Marci's grandparents, parents, siblings, aunts, uncles and cousins were a folksy lot who enjoyed simple pleasures.

The most daring escapade she could remember from her youth was sneaking Mollie May, the neighbor's heifer, into McDonald's grocery story and hanging a sign around her neck with the lyrics to the children's song *Old McDonald Had A Farm*. When Mr. McDonald arrived at the store in the morning, Mollie had eaten her way through an entire shelf of potato chips and bags of Reese's Peanut Butter Cups.

As punishment for their misdeeds, Marci and her friends had to wash the offensively scented after effects of Mollie's binge eating from the grocery store floors. She claimed it had taken weeks to get the odor of cow manure out of her nose.

One of Marci's favorite stories, which she encouraged Cat to repeat many times and to as many people as possible, featured the *capo di tutti capi* who ruled the neighborhood where Cat grew up. His friends called him Blackie, and Cat always said that she was never sure whether it was due to his unrepentant soul or the god-awful modified afro toupee he always wore.

Cat was quick to point out to everyone within hearing distance that they would never have known what career path her father's patients had chosen to follow just by looking at them. Sure, there were a few who were caught in a time warp—duck's ass haircuts, tight fitting rolled-sleeve tee shirts, cigarettes dangling from their lips and hunks of wire and handguns on their belts. Those visual aids might be dead giveaways, but for the most part, they looked just like everyone else.

At this point in the story telling, Marci always added a quote by Sherlock Holmes, her and Cat's favorite fictional detective. "The world is full of obvious things which nobody by any chance ever observes."

"Old Sherlock was correct. The first time I met Red...," Cat illustrated her point, "… he was standing in our driveway smoking a cigarette. I was returning home from walking, Sheikira, our domesticated wolf, and he stopped me to comment on what an unusual and beautiful animal she was. We talked for a while and, when I finally went into the house, I did so thinking 'What a nice guy. And cute!' After office hours, I mentioned him to my dad. His response was about as curt as one could get. 'Don't ever talk to him again!'"

"Papa bear was protecting his cub. Did you say, 'wolf? I don't think you ever told me that before. How could that be?'"

"Yes, my father was being protective, and I did say wolf. As for whether I've ever told you that before, now you know why I contribute to all those wolf conservation organizations. Anyway, I argued with my dad that Red was '… such a nice guy,' but he was adamant that I stay far away from him. He even threatened to fire me and make me get a real job, but I didn't care. I just kept pressuring him to tell me why.

**April 1996:**

"Come on, dad. You can't just tell me I can't talk to somebody without telling me why. That only makes me want to talk to him more."

"You have always been much too stubborn and independent for your own good, Cat. Why can't you just trust me on this? Red is not someone you should want for a friend."

"I don't want him for a friend. I just want to know why you don't want me to have him as a friend."

"You're just like your mother. You can never just accept what I say without demanding all the details. Okay. Red is an enforcer. To put it more succinctly, he's a hit man."

"Really? A hit man? Well, I guess having a home office really does have its pros and cons… pun intended, Dad."

"Sounds like you were getting an education on a number of different levels. Did your father ever tell you who Red had killed?" Adult Marci was just as intrigued by Red as had been teenaged Cat.

"He didn't have to tell me. A few weeks passed with no sign of Red. Then, one night on the evening news, his face filled the television screen. According to the report, he had entered a bar and used a shotgun to blow the heads off a few of the patrons."

"Your father must have had a shit fit. I'll bet he gave you an earful about questioning his judgment."

"Actually, no. He didn't say anything. Red was caught by the police a few days later and, at his arraignment, despite handcuffs and shackles, managed to jump through a second story window at the courthouse and escape. The police were asking for help in finding him and a reward was being offered, but the last we heard, no one had ever turned him in."

"Didn't your father feel threatened by these men?"

"Not at all. They knew my dad was a straight up guy. He wanted nothing to do with their lives outside his office. He was there to treat their illnesses and injuries. Nothing else."

"But weren't they worried that your dad would overhear something or say something that could get them arrested? He was a police physician."

"Dad never asked questions beyond their health issues, and they never offered information. On any given day, there were just as many cops in our waiting room as there were not so law abiding citizens. They all knew each other and, assuming there were no outstanding arrest warrants, they treated each other like long lost friends."

"I guess it was no different than now," Marci commented. "We know who the perverts and scumbags are in our community but, without evidence, we can't do a damn thing to put them behind bars."

"Yup. My dad said that he would rather have them sitting in our waiting room than out committing a crime."

# CHAPTER TWO

*A* shiny black Cadillac Esplanade, its engine so perfectly tuned that it barely made a sound, glided its way along a makeshift road leading deep into the Florida Everglades. Upon entering a small clearing, the car stopped and three men exited. If not for the headlights on the vehicle, darkness would have completely engulfed the men, making them invisible even to each other.

One of the men was bound and gagged. His face showed evidence of a beating—his left eye swollen shut, his nose smashed, bleeding and flattened against his cheek. One wore a cheap suit bought off the rack at Men's Warehouse. He held the beaten man's shoulder in a firm grip preventing him from moving. The third man was elegantly attired and appeared ready for an evening of fine dining.

Vincent Policastro was tall, imposing, with a full head of silver hair and hard facial features dominated by a classic Roman nose. He had a confident air that intimidated even the most self-assured and successful of his associates. All of his clothing, from underwear and socks to neckties and handkerchiefs, was made in Chiaia, the elegant waterfront neighborhood in Naples, Italy considered to be superior to London's Savile Row.

Chiaia was home to the noble house of Rubinacci Napoli, a multigenerational family business revered as innovators in the design of classic Italian menswear for nearly a century. Vincent's two and three piece suits, which numbered 150, were black—the only color he ever wore—and specially made by Rubinacci himself. When Vincent entered a room wearing a Rubinacci original, his body language fairly shouted, "You can't touch me."

Rubinacci Napoli made each of Vincent's suit jackets to hide the presence of his Beretta 96A1. The lethal handgun was worn in a specially designed leather shoulder holster and was well-concealed by Vincent's finely chiseled musculature. On this night, the gun would remain hidden from prying eyes.

The beaten man looked at Vincent and tried to talk through the cloth shoved deep into his mouth. He was obviously frantic; a pleading tone evident even though his words were indistinguishable from the sobs that threatened to choke him. Vincent was unmoved. With barely a nod of his head, he signaled the gunman to carry out his mission. The bullet that shattered the kneeling man's head sent a spray of blood toward Vincent, dotting his face, shirt, tie and jacket with red. He did not flinch.

The gunman picked up the shovel that had been placed against the fender of the Cadillac. He dug a hole into which he pushed the dead man's body. Then, he walked to the trunk of the car and opened it. He removed a garment bag which he held up for his boss to see. Vincent slowly removed his jacket, shirt and tie. He used his shirt to wipe the blood from his face.

Each of Vincent Policastro's suit jackets and all of his dress shirts had a personalized label inside the collar on which was typed V. Policastro/Naples/and the date the article of clothing was made. The gunman handed him a knife which he used to cut the labels from inside his jacket and the collar of his shirt. These he placed in the pocket of his pants while dropping the rest of the clothing to the ground. Then, he dressed unhurriedly, not bothered by the army of mosquitoes that hovered over his head but never landed.

When he was neatly attired, Vincent once again nodded to the gunman, who returned the garment bag and the shovel to the trunk and slammed the lid. The gunman picked up the discarded clothing and a container of gasoline that had been placed near the car. He dropped the jacket, shirt and tie on top of the dead man in the hole and poured in the gasoline. Then, he lit a match and dropped that into the hole as well.

Together, the gunman and Vincent stood side by side and watched as the fire destroyed all traces of their crime. When the flames were nothing but embers, they drove back the way they had come unseen except for the alligators that watched silently from the tall reeds, paying their respects as only one predator can do for another.

Those who knew Vincent Policastro well would have disagreed with Mark Twain's assertion that "Clothes make the man. Naked people have little or no influence on society." Where Vincent was concerned, clothes merely disguised the true nature of the beast within. Even naked, he was to be feared. At 63, he controlled one of the biggest and most powerful organized crime families on the east coast. His multi-billion dollar kingdom was ruled from a zen-inspired mansion in Manalapan, Florida, where he was a familiar face on the boards of some high-profile charities and at fundraisers frequented by the social elite of Snob Island—Cat's and Marci's name for Palm Beach.

# CHAPTER THREE

The weeks leading up to Cat's wedding to Kevin Kavanagh were hectic but not for the usual reasons. Rather than keeping the appointments she had made for dress fittings and being focused on writing her vows, completing the seating chart, and ordering flower arrangements and favors, Cat spent every minute of her spare time pursuing leads in the Ribbon Rapist case and spreading her message of awareness to women's organizations. She and Marci had appearances booked for an entire year.

The Ribbon Rapist -- that was how Cat referred to the man who had combed his victims' hair into ponytails atop their heads and tied them with colorful streamers of cotton —the same man who had raped her in 2007. She refused to call him by his given name or to refer to him as *my rapist* out of deference to the other women who had been victimized by him and, in particular, to the two women who were still missing.

Every Wednesday morning, either Cat or Marci stopped by the State's Attorney's office for a quick catch meeting on open cases. On one particular Wednesday, Cat arrived back at the station to find Kevin standing in the parking lot holding a big, pink bakery box.

"Hey. What are you doing here?"

"Today was our cake tasting. You weren't there so I'm here."

"Oh, my god, Kevin. I'm so sorry. I completely forgot."

"That was obvious." The scowl on Kevin's face softened into a look of resignation. "It's okay. I know you have a lot on your mind. The baker gave me samples for you to try. I liked the vanilla cream, but I think you'll like the chocolate fudge. She said we could do both layers if we wanted."

"I can't taste them now. I'm late for a speech at the Women's Advocacy Group. Marci is already there."

"Cat, we're getting married. The wedding is important to me. I'd like it to be important to you, too." The scowl was back on Kevin's face.

When Cat arrived at the little house in Northwood Village which the WAG called home, Marci was pacing the front porch impatiently.

"I thought you weren't coming. I've been trying to text you."

"I had a cake emergency. Plus, I don't text and drive. Let's go inside. I'll explain later."

While the moderator gave her welcoming speech, Cat and Marci reviewed their notes backstage. They had their relay act down pat... Cat first, then Marci, then back to Cat. Even so, prior to every speech, Cat got butterflies in her stomach. The Ribbon Rapist was not a fond memory for her.

Robert Bridgeman had raped and tortured five young women including Cat. He murdered four of them. Cat had been his first and, for some unexplained reason, he had left her alive. Perhaps, it was because he did not know she was a police officer. Perhaps, he was still unsure of himself. First-time predators often test the waters before becoming fully engaged in their crimes. Whatever the reason, the other four women had not been as fortunate. The bodies of Miss Pink and Miss Green – Bridgeman tied his victims' hair with colorful ribbons and tattooed the nicknames he gave them on his back -- were resting at Queen of Peace Cemetery, but Miss Purple and Miss Orange were still missing. Cat had promised that she would not rest until the women had been found and received proper burials. Their families deserved closure as well.

As a constant reminder of her promise to never give up, two 14 inch purple ribbons and two equal sized orange ribbons hung on the bulletin board in the office Cat shared with Marci. Hanging next to them was a photo of the tattoo on Bridgeman's back taken at the time Cat shot and killed him. The tattoo listed the colorful names he gave his victims: Miss Pink, Miss Green, Miss Purple, Miss Orange and Miss Blue – Cat Leigh.

Surviving a brutal beating and rape had made Cat painfully cognizant that every moment of every day was to be cherished. Whenever she and Marci spoke to members of women's groups and civic organizations about the need for constant vigilance when out in public, they made sure to talk about the realities of life… not the fantasies that were often touted in tourist guides and by politicians seeking re-election.

Recently, Cat and Marci had given a speech at a networking luncheon for female executives and, at it, Cat had been verbally attacked by a few women who felt her message to "… constantly be aware" was victim blaming.

"Why the hell should women have to reflexively think about self-defense in a damn supermarket parking lot five minutes from home in a decent neighborhood?"

Cat set the speaker straight very quickly.

"No woman deserves to be raped. Choosing to go naked through the streets does not qualify a female as being rape worthy. Nothing a woman does… no manner of behavior justifies abuse. But -- and there is always a but – you must be prepared for the possibility of danger even if you are just going shopping at your friendly neighborhood grocery store. You must accept the fact that you're not deserving to be raped means nothing to a rapist. Being impaired or distracted in any way – whether by alcohol, restrictive clothing, a mental grocery list, your children, anything – could put you in danger.

It is true that women all over the world should be able to go, do and dress as they want without fear of assault. But we don't live between the pages of a story book. This is not a fairy tale. This is real life and, here, the princess often wakes up brutally beaten -- if she is lucky to wake up at all. And why? Because she chose to protect herself with rhetoric rather than reason."

Marci picked up the conversation knowing that what she was about to say would be difficult for Cat to convey without getting emotional.

"Recently, Cat and I sat in on the three-hour interrogation of a rapist who had pummeled his victim with his fists until her nose was broken. He had also held a gun to her head to guarantee cooperation.

Trust me, this guy didn't give a damn about women's rights. He was only interested in his own wants and needs, and he brought that gun along to make sure he wasn't denied them. I can guarantee you one thing... in a battle between a weapon and any mottos or slogans proclaiming a woman's right to do as she pleases, the weapon will always win."

Right at this point, another woman spoke up.

"The idea that women must be vigilant 24 hours a day/seven days a week is unrealistic and abusive. That's never going to happen because it would mean that women have to give up the freedom to live a normal life. If we don't take the precautions you suggest and something happens, we will be blamed for the outcome. You're basically making us prisoners of circumstance and you're asking us to wear mental orange jumpsuits as a constant reminder that we aren't actually free."

Cat struggled to keep the frustration out of her voice. She had heard these arguments many times in the past, but the refusal to accept danger as a constant in our lives always caused knots to form in her stomach. "I have never said that women can't dress as they choose. I've never said women can't go where they want to go or behave in a way that suits them. I ask that each of you be prepared for what might happen anywhere and anytime so that, should danger present itself, you can better protect yourselves. Everyone is a target at some time in their life. You must decide whether you want to be a hard target or a soft target."

Here Cat paused to let her words sink in. She knew that most of her audience would not understand her reference to soft and hard targets. When the murmurs subsided, she continued speaking.

"If you want to reduce the chances of being a victim, you must consider all the variables. A soft target is a person who is relatively unprotected... vulnerable mostly due to their own choices. A hard target is someone who takes precautions. For example, one person... male or female... is sitting in their car in a nearly deserted parking lot texting and talking on their phone while listening to the radio. The car window is open and they are unaware... disinterested... in anything happening beyond the confines of their automobile. Another person is behaving exactly the same way only their windows and doors are locked. Who do you think a criminal will target?

It is a fact that we grow stronger and wiser due to the experiences in our lives. We can also grow wiser learning from other people's experiences. The best way to stay safe is to think... always think before venturing out into the world even if you are only venturing to the end of the driveway to put out your trash."

No matter where Cat and Marci spoke, their speeches did not vary much one from the next. They ended their appearance at the Women's Advocacy Group just as they did every appearance. Cat held her arm up high, the underside facing the audience so that everyone could see the teal blue ribbon tattoo on her wrist.

"I would rather that the only adornment you wear on your wrist is a bracelet... not a deep scar and a tattoo which for me are constant reminders that I very nearly did not survive a brush with death. I would rather that your name not wind up inked on the shoulder blade of a rapist like a notch on a bedpost or a mark on a gun grip the way gunslingers used to celebrate their kills. The only way you can guarantee your own safety is to take responsibility for it."

Cat and Marci made their way to the exit door in silence. These appearances, as well-rehearsed as they were, took an emotional toll on both of them. Suddenly, they heard footsteps rapidly approaching from behind and someone calling out Cat's name.

"Detective Leigh! Detective Leigh! Wait!"

Cat and Marci turned to see a member of the Women's Advocacy Group running toward them.

"I was afraid I had missed you. Someone left this envelope for you. It was on top of the guest book by the entry door to the dining room."

Cat took the envelope from the woman's outstretched hand. "Thank you."

"No problem. I'm just glad I caught up with you. Great speech. I'm sorry for what happened to you."

"Thanks."

Cat looked down at the envelope. Written in magic marker on the front were the words:

URGENT! FOR DETECTIVE JESSICA LEIGH

She tore the envelope open and removed a single sheet of paper onto which letters from a newspaper had been pasted.

Marci read the message while looking over Cat's shoulder:

*Madam Currie discovered polonium in 1898 – by mistake. I don't make mistakes.*

Marci's whisper sounded like a rocket exploding. "Holy shit!"

Cat called to the departing WAG member. "Hey. Did you happen to see who left this?"

"No, Detective. I'm sorry. No one was stationed at the back of the room once lunch was served."

"Okay. Thanks."

Cat and Marci stared at each other for a moment, each gathering their thoughts.

"Cameras. Are there security cameras in this place?" Cat was already moving toward the little office off the center hallway.

Returning to the headquarters a few hours later, Cat turned the envelope – now secured in a plastic evidence bag – over to forensics. There was always a chance that a fingerprint... even a partial fingerprint... might be found.

"No cameras. Who doesn't have security cameras these days." Cat drummed her fingers on the desktop in frustration.

"I'm not surprised. What need do they have for enhanced security?" Marci sighed as she pulled a chair up next to Cat.

"True. There really wasn't anything to steal unless you happen to like artificial flower arrangements. They don't keep money on premises and the few computers they own aren't worth much."

"Their members, all volunteers, mostly work from home which keeps overhead low and allows the organization to donate most of the money they raise to charity." Marci read from a brochure published by the WAG. "Nice group of women."

"Yes. They are." Cat paused to collect her thoughts. "We need to talk to Brandon Hanson. I've got a feeling about him. Even though that bomb threat at FAU turned out to be innocuous, he just seems like... well, a ticking time bomb."

"I found the discussion with his adviser at the college very interesting. And that poem he sent to his teacher saying he wanted to bring him a gift. That was a veiled threat if I ever read one."

*Kill them with kindness*
*That's what I say*

*Those who don't listen*
*Kill them another way*

"Yeah. And it would be difficult to misunderstand the meaning behind, 'I have absolutely no doubt in my mind that I want to blow up the school.'"

"I can't believe they didn't have him arrested. Political correctness be damned! He could have injured a lot of people."

Putting further thoughts of Brandon Hanson aside for the moment, Cat and Marci quietly filed their reports on the day's events. Stomachs growling, they signed out of the precinct at 6:00 pm. It had been another long day.

As they made their way to their cars, Marci grabbed Cat by the arm. "Okay. I've been waiting all day. What the hell is a cake emergency?"

"It was nothing. Forget it."

"I'm not forgetting it. I want to know why you're so quiet. It's more than just the mysterious envelope." Marci stood in front of the door to the parking lot, blocking Cat's exit.

"Remember last week when I forgot to meet Kevin at the florist to choose the center pieces for the reception?"

"Yeah. He was kinda pissed."

"And he was again today when I didn't show up at the bakery to taste the wedding cakes."

"Uh oh. What did he say?"

"He said he liked the vanilla cream cake best. I liked the chocolate. We're getting both."

# CHAPTER FOUR

*O*n the morning of her wedding, Cat promised herself and Marci that she would put the need to "… always think of the danger" out of her mind for the day, but she did it under duress. Marci caught her looking through the murder book on the Governor Gardner case while she was having her hair done just a few hours before the ceremony was to take place.

In police lingo, a murder book is the case file of a crime under investigation. Typically, murder books include crime scene photographs, eye witness-based sketches, autopsy and forensic reports, transcripts of the detectives' notes and witness interviews. A murder book is the bible of crime fighting.

When Marci entered the room where Cat was getting her hair done, Cat tried to hide the loose leaf binder under a People Magazine, but Marci saw its blue edges and knew that her partner was still hard at work.

"Give me that," Marci demanded of Cat as she pulled the book out of Cat's lap. "This is your wedding day. No one will think less of you if you think happy thoughts for a few hours."

"Okay. I promise," Cat said, eyes twinkling. "All I will think about is Kevin and our wedding and, of course, the honeymoon that awaits."

Even knowing what she knew, Cat still believed a little bit in fairy tales and wanted her day to be perfect in every way… and it was. The reception was a simple yet elegant affair held at the beautiful Breakers West Clubhouse.

The bride wore a dress of her own design… a form fitting Grecian gown which draped her body from shoulders to floor in delicate layers white, ecru and cream chiffon. Despite having missed many fitting appointments, the dress fit perfectly. Its V-neck was cut low in front and high on one leg. A band of crystals under her breasts emphasized the perfect peaks that were just barely hidden by the fabric.

Her long blonde hair was twisted into a flower-filled knot at the back of her head. On her feet were crystal studded high-heeled sandals that added another four inches to her already 5' 10" frame. No veil or hat detracted from the beautiful face God had created. The professional makeup artist hired for the occasion used a light hand to enhance already high cheek bones, big blue eyes and naturally voluptuous lips. Cat had refused to let her lighten the two inch raised scar on the side of her neck where a machete blade had left an indelible imprint.

Marci was, of course, her matron of honor and two friends who were also co-workers served as bridesmaids. Four-year-old Sonora Leslie, Marci's daughter, was the flower girl. The two young daughters of another friend were junior bridesmaids.

The ceremony was originally planned to take place in the garden under the bright blue skies that were typical in Florida most of the year. Mother Nature, however, decided that a little sprinkle of liquid sunshine was needed to keep the grass green and the flowers blooming so, without warning, storm clouds gathered over the guests forcing them to take refuge inside. The staff at Breakers West quickly brought in the flowered trellis under which Cat and Kevin were to take their vows and set it up in an empty meeting room along with enough chairs for all to be comfortable. When the processional march began and Sonora Leslie began her walk down the aisle, dropping rose petals along the way, everyone forgot about the thunder crashing against the roof.

Then Cat entered on her father's arm and a hush fell over the room. Yes, she looked beautiful, but it wasn't her physical appearance that brought tears to the guests' eyes. Everyone remembered that just a few short years ago, Cat had resembled the Elephant Man – her body and face battered and bruised, her nose broken, her lips and mouth cut, and her neck sliced by the sharp blade of a machete. Now, she stood before them, healed in body and soul, a vision of peace and contentment. There was joy on her face and that joy was reflected in the faces of all who loved her and wished her well on this her special day.

At the cocktail hour following the ceremony, family and friends mingled and shared *getting to know you* stories. Marci, who had only met Cat's parents a few times, was anxious to talk to her father and learn more about the people he had cared for before retiring from his medical practice. When the opportunity arose, she cornered Dr. Leigh and asked about Blackie and his gang of thieves.

"Dr. Leigh, Cat talks all the time about the interesting characters you cared for in your practice. I love hearing those stories. They make good reference points when we are investigating crimes like the current Policastro case. Cat has mentioned two guys... brothers, I think... who really fascinate me."

"You mean the Cafasso brothers... John and Dennis."

"That's them. Cat told me a story about one stabbing the other."

"John was the more volatile of the two. He was always unpredictable. One year, he stabbed Dennis in an argument over whether they should have hamburgers or steak at their Fourth of July barbecue."

"How serious was the wound?" Marci hung on to Dr. Leigh's words with rapt attention.

"Serious enough that I had to drive him to the hospital. Of course, Dennis didn't want to get his brother in any trouble so he told the emergency room doctor that he cut himself on a piece of broken glass. It was obvious the doctor didn't believe his story, but he was smart enough to just stitch the wound and send Dennis home.

If you ever saw this guy, you would understand why the doctor was intimidated. The next day, the brothers were acting like nothing had happened."

"Are you sure you don't want to write a screenplay? It would be an Academy Award winner."

"I've thought about it. Maybe someday… when I'm sure they're all dead and won't come looking for me."

"Did anything else happen with them?"

"Lots of things. I remember that a few months later, John got injured on his legitimate job. He and Dennis owned a wholesale beverage company. They sold large quantities of beer and soft drinks for private parties and public events. John came into my dad's office complaining that he had excruciating pain in his back, neck and shoulders. He wanted to file a workman's comp case and needed an attorney.

I never liked recommending one particular lawyer over another even if I felt he or she was best for the case. That way, if the case did not settle in favor of a patient, I couldn't be held responsible. And, besides, it was illegal to do that."

"But you wouldn't be responsible one way or the other."

"You know that and I know that, but we're not talking about reasonable and rational people here, especially in John Cafasso's case. I always avoided offering suggestions by giving anyone who asked for references the names of a few attorneys we trusted. The lawyer John chose happened to be my best friend."

"I get the feeling things didn't go well."

"The case proceeded to arbitration, but John wasn't satisfied with the amount of money offered. He insisted on going to court and totally disregarded his attorney's warning that the insurance company would waste no effort in proving his injuries less severe than he claimed.

Came the day of the trial and, sure enough, the lawyers for the insurance company produced a video of John carrying heavy wooden crates of soda bottles and kegs of beer. Bye, bye settlement. He was angry, but he was angry with the attorney, not himself.

In a fit of temper, John stormed into my office and threatened to kill the lawyer. Knowing that John kept a baseball bat that was sawed into a club and wrapped in razor wire in his car, I was pretty worried about my friend."

"What did you do?" Marci's face was etched with worry.

"I offered John a drink, which calmed his nerves. Then, I called Blackie and told him what had happened. At Blackie's request, I kept John occupied until he arrived."

"Oh! Oh! Then what happened."

"Watching someone get the shit kicked out of him in the movies is nothing like watching in real life. There's no slow motion. Things happen so quickly that you can neither prepare yourself nor get out of the way."

~

**January 1997:**

"This is some damned good scotch, Doc. Who'd you hafta highjack to get a bottle?"

"You know I don't do…"

Like Satan with hemorrhoids, Blackie came through the door, his coat open and flapping like big black wings as he marched up behind John and hit him so hard in the back of the head that the glass broke and cut into the bridge of his nose.

"You fucking son of a bitch. Do you never learn? How many times have I told you not to threaten people who are not in our line of work?"

"But, boss, that shit lawyer cost me a fortune. I didn't get a dime and now I have to pay him for losing the case. Plus, I'll probably get fined by the court for bringing a frivolous lawsuit or some such crap."

Blood was streaming down John's face as Blackie lifted him out of his chair by the shirt and delivered a few well-placed punches to his stomach and chin.

"If one hair on that attorney's head is out of place, if he gets hit by a car, if a hurricane blows through and destroys his home, this is nothing compared to what I will do to you. Get the hell out of my sight."

~

"John didn't fight back? Didn't argue with Blackie?" Marci's eyes were as large as saucers.

"Nobody argued with Blackie..." Dr. Leigh said, "... not if they valued their life. The Hammer escorted John out of the office. Blackie extended a hand in thanks and he left. I never saw John again, but I did hear stories... scary stories that I won't repeat just in case he knows how to use Google maps."

"Did Cat see it happen?"

"No. But she heard it all. She was inside our family room which was just on the other side of the office. Truthfully, she was pretty scared but it did have one beneficial outcome."

"What was that?"

"She lost all interest in Red Ritchie. I know she told you about him."

"She did! Have to admit he sounded divine and your practice was definitely not dull."

"I don't want you to get the wrong impression, Marci. I had many more average patients than I did strange characters. Every night in the waiting room, they would share stories of spouses, kids, pets... you name it. Anyone listening would never suspect what they did for a living. That's why Cat always tells people that there is a real danger in talking to strangers."

When dinner was announced, Marci reluctantly let Dr. Leigh return to his wife's side. She took her place in the processional line along with the other attendants and the bride and groom.

Each of the male investigators in the homicide division of the PBSO played a part in the wedding. Detectives Maurice "Moe" Di Lorenzo and Pete Shonto were ushers. Detective Damian Mack and Sgt. Paulie Padrone were greeters. Many others, like Officer Keith McKinney and Medical Examiner Mark "G" Geschwer, begged to toast their colleague and share stories of her bravery. Since they had all witnessed Cat's battered face and body after the assault, her wedding was as much a celebration of healing for them as it was for her.

Marci made a little toast of her own, telling everyone how Cat and Kevin had met at Moe's Southwest... a meeting she had witnessed and pronounced blessed by fate. Then, Sonora Leslie and the two young bridesmaids did an impromptu song and dance routine which captivated everyone and added a level of merriment to the festivities not usually felt at weddings.

By the time dinner was served, all the guests were relaxed and looking forward to tripping the light fantastic on the dance floor. The only time the music stopped was when the speeches were being given. Those who spoke celebrated the couple's love for each other, Cat's bravery in facing her attacker and her strength of character.

A grand time was had by all... right up to the moment a gunshot was heard coming from the lake area behind the clubhouse. Thinking the explosive sound was a firecracker, Cat and Marci did not respond with their usual speed. Only the quick movements of the waiters, who put down the dinners they were serving and rushed from the reception hall put everyone on notice that something was wrong. The Sheriff's Office detectives who were guests at the wedding signaled to Cat and Marci to "... stay put," while they went to investigate. When they did not return, the bride and her matron of honor knew it was time to change their clothes and go to work.

The body of Gamaliel Cohen was found floating face down in the brown waters of the man-made pond that marked the 10$^{th}$ hole of the Breakers West golf course. Andy, the 10 foot long and roughly 270 pound alligator who had lived on the golf course for many years, watched from a nearby bank. His presence prevented any attempts to wade in and pull the slowly sinking body to shore.

The golf course manager, whose responsibility it was to keep the pond mosquito and dead body free, pulled a small fiberglass motor boat out of its hiding place in the tall reeds. He offered it to Detectives Damian Mack and Maurice Di Lorenzo of the PBSO's Homicide Division.

"You have any idea who this guy is?" Moe DiLorenzo asked the course manager.

"Yes, sir. It's Gamalial Cohen. He lives here at the club."

"What's his name?" Moe hated unusual names… first, last or otherwise. He found them pretentious and always felt embarrassed if he didn't say them properly.

"Gamalial. It's pronounced Gama… like gamma rays only with one M… and leel… like real only with an L. It's a Jewish name."

"Aren't Aaron and Adam Jewish names? Why can't people just name their kids something simple?"

Mack was a twice divorced former Marine with a biting wit and a fear of roaches, especially the flying variety. His good friend and new partner, Moe Di Lorenzo, was a rotund fellow who avoided the beach, the ocean, a pool… anything that required him undressing and exposing what he called his "blubber guts." Every diet he had ever gone on had only succeeded in adding more weight to his hefty size.

"Don't worry about it, Moe. I'll take care of what's his name. You take care of the alligator." Mack knew exactly what Moe's reaction would be to that suggestion.

"Why'd it have to be an alligator? I hate alligators. You go." Moe stepped away from the water's edge, an unspoken acknowledgment that his weight was too much for the little boat, and he had no intention of becoming Andy's evening meal. "No point in you having to pull two bodies from the pond."

Damian Mack steered the boat into the middle of the lake and slipped a rope around the body. As he worked the length of hemp over Gamalial Cohen's head and under his arms, he kept one eye on Andy, who had begun to move toward the water's edge, no longer satisfied with being a spectator. Like pebbles thrown into a pond, Andy's body sent ripples across the surface. The closer the ripples got to the boat, the quicker Detective Mack worked.

Gamaliel Cohen, Esq. was a much respected and feared attorney. He was also the personal and business representative for a very influential and powerful family. Along with his wife and two young sons, he lived in a large house on the seventh hole of the golf course—a 7,200 square foot, five bedroom/five and a half bath two story home that was beyond envy worthy in a community that was filled with enviable residences. Gamaliel Cohen was as close to being a made man as one could get without actually being one. He was highly respected in the organization but, not being of Italian descent, he was excluded from receiving the dubious title of *uomo* d'onore – man of honor. The family and business he represented – Vincent Policastro's empire.

# CHAPTER FIVE

*A*merican Airlines flight 1819 out of LaGuardia landed at Palm Beach International Airport at 11:58 pm on the evening of October 17th. Vincent did not go straight to the hotel where Maria was waiting for him. Instead, he stopped by Crotone Moving Company in Boynton Beach. Crotone Moving had been started many years before in the town of Petilia de Policastro in the province of Crotone, in Calabria, Italy, by Vincent's paternal grandfather. Settled in the Byzantine era, the town was believed to have been the home of Pope Anterus, who was the Bishop of Rome from November 21, 235 to his death in 236. Anterus, who was thought to have been of Greek descent, was considered by many to be a freed slave.

Vincent could not have cared less about the origins of his ancestral home. He christened his company Crotone Moving as a subtle middle finger to the American federal authorities. His deceased grandfather was a founding member of the 'Ndrangheta, an organized crime family centered in Calabria. Despite not being as famous abroad as the Sicilian Mafia, the 'Ndrangheta became the most powerful crime syndicate in Italy in the late 1990s and early 2000s. While commonly tied together with the Sicilian Mafia, the 'Ndrangheta operated independently from them. It had been estimated that the organization's narcotics trafficking, extortion and money laundering activities accounted for, at least, 3% of Italy's gross domestic product. Since the 1950s, the organization had spread towards Northern Italy and worldwide.

Nothing pissed Vincent off more than to hear the name of his company pronounced "croton," like the plant, by people totally oblivious to ethnic and cultural diversity. The only thing the two words had in common was that the oil extracted from the seeds of the croton plant were often used in herbal medicines as a violent purgative to treat severe constipation. The 'Ndrangheta could also be viewed as a "violent purgative" as they favored emptying the pockets and savings accounts of northern Italy's rich by kidnapping and ransoming family members... and the possibility of mutilation and death was always a part of the negotiations.

When Vincent arrived at Crotone Moving, two of his trusted henchmen were playing dice on the sidewalk despite the late hour. Joey "JoJo" Jericho, who Vincent referred to as "cretino," was a wiry, tattooed simpleton. He was 30 going on 13. Frankie "the Fist" Fortunato was in his 50's. He had an intelligent face which stood in stark contrast to his powerfully thick neck and arms, broad shoulders and missing three fingers on his left hand, the result of an unplanned meeting between three members of a rival family and a table saw.

While Frankie was down on one knee making a shot, Joey was standing a few feet away feeding bits of a Big Mac to a stray dog. The dog, a friendly, flea bitten mutt, was obviously used to getting his midnight meal from Joey.

Frankie looked at his partner with disgust. "You realize the boss is going to kill you and him if he sees that mutt hanging around here."

"He won't see him. I'll chase him away."

"You better hope Vincent doesn't chase you away... permanently."

"I'm just being nice. What's the big deal?"

"We're about to find out. Here's the boss now."

In a panic, Joey ran to the alley at the side of the building and threw the remains of the sandwich as far as he could. The dog raced after it. "That was close."

"What was the rush if it was no big deal?" Frankie taunted Joey, knowing that just the opposite was true.

Vincent approached the two men from across the street, walking slowly and with impossible-to-miss pain. Joey and Frankie watched him maneuver cautiously up onto the curb.

"Before you ask, I hurt my back. Got into a little tussle with a hussy at The Firehouse. She got too aggressive using my hose to put out her flames."

"You better hope the wife doesn't find out."

"How's she going to find out, asshole? You think I'm going to tell her when I get home?" Vincent smacked Joey on the back of the head. "If I even suspect she knows, I'll come looking for you and that mutt you've been feeding. I'll use you both for target practice. How many frickin' times have I told you to get rid of him?"

"He just hangs around, boss."

"Don't butter my ass with bullshit. I can smell your crap a mile away. It's late and I want to go home. Frankie, where's Ernie? He was supposed to meet us here."

"He's on his way, boss. Said he was following up on Johnny Porco, the jadrool from Miami who owes us 30 big ones. You want me to call our guy who works on the Dolphins? He's a master with massage."

"No. I'm leaving. Tell Ernie I'll call him tomorrow. You...," Vincent pointed to Joey, "... get rid of the mongrel or I'll get rid of you."

Frankie bent down to pick up the dice, the action preventing Vincent from seeing the troubled look on his face. Joey was courting death... everyone knew it. When Frankie looked up, the dog was back and taking a leak against the side of the building. His sigh was one of relief that, at least for tonight, only urine would need to be washed off the sidewalk and not Joey's blood.

Vincent made his way back to his car, hobbling as he crossed the street. Joey's comment about Maria had caused some troubling thoughts to surface in his mind. The men who did Vincent's bidding were devoid of conscience, but it was Maria he feared. He was well aware of her expertise with a gun and her intolerance of his philandering ways. He hoped fate never put those two realities in the same place at the same time. He recited his own version of "Bless me, Father, for I have sinned" all the way to the Ritz Carlton.

# CHAPTER SIX

*V*incent's wife, Maria—somewhere between 40 and don't ask—was petite and beyond beautiful. Her shoulder length auburn hair sparked with aurulent lights reflecting off the heavy gold jewelry she wore on her wrists and around her neck. She preferred diamonds the size of moth balls in her ears and golf balls on her fingers.

Seen from the rear, the sight of Maria's departing derrière was enough to make grown men grab their chests and utter words like *Madonna mia.* From the front, their reaction to her shapely legs, tiny waist and big breasts was an obvious bulge in the area between their waist and thighs. Some men would grab that erect appendage in a show of appreciation. Fools that they were, these men had ignored Vincent's oft-voiced warning that they would need to sit down to pee if they dared to touch her. A few had actually been forced to do that.

Born to the mean streets of Newark, New Jersey, Maria Angelina Sacco was 18 when she crossed paths with made-man Vincent Policastro, twenty years her senior. The meeting was unplanned but fortuitous for both of them. While attempting to pick Vincent's pocket at a local social club, Maria got caught in the act. Vincent grabbed and painfully twisted her arm, forcing her to her knees. The defiance in her deep green eyes as she looked up at him captured his heart. The fierce power in his eyes captured her heart. A wedding attended by 300 of their closest friends and enemies was held six months later.

During their marriage, Maria had grown accustomed to the best the world had to offer. Her strong willed-temperament, a challenge even for her more strong-willed husband, guaranteed that she got whatever she wanted and rightfully so. She had proven herself to be not only a beautiful piece of arm candy and insatiable lover but a creative and innovative criminal master mind as well. The lack of a high school diploma was not a hindrance. Maria was a mathematical genius with a photographic memory. Proof of her abilities could be found by asking anyone who had played and lost at cards whenever she was at the table.

Rather than the normal bill and coo that lovers shared, Vincent's and Maria's pillow talk entailed plans for expanding their "family" and their fortunes. On the third Sunday of every month, the Policastro's reserved a penthouse suite at the luxurious Ritz Carlton Hotel located a few minutes from their home. The reason was a high stakes poker game.

According to the hype on their website, the Ritz Carlton is "... an exclusive island city that sits at the intersection of wealth, power and international style. It is the epicenter of cache and culture and, as such, a gathering place of exquisitely sensuous and playful people, drawing everyone from Hollywood stars to heads of state." Nowhere do the marketing geniuses mention high-stakes Texas Hold 'Em with people who use semi-automatic weapons as toothpicks.

Vincent didn't play cards. His wife, however, was a shark extraordinaire. The men who came to challenge her winning streak almost always allowed ego to override skill. This macho mentality resulted in Maria becoming a very rich woman in her own right. Without Vincent's knowledge, each month she squirreled away a minimum of $40,000 in a secret New York bank account. The $20,000 she didn't deposit, she shared with her husband. The reasons for her actions were known only to her.

Maria's unending winning streak puzzled everyone but Vincent. One of the things he loved most about his wife was the ability to remember minute details—including every card that had been dealt. She was an amateur psychologist who was quick to recognize a liar from the first introduction and a genius at reading tells. If Butch Zito drank his Courvoisier quickly, Maria knew his pockets were near to empty. If he drank slowly, he had a winning hand… or so he thought. When Jimmy, the Saint, Santino began spitting phlegm into his handkerchief, it meant frustration was setting in. Since he was a volatile man, Maria intentionally lost the next hand to him. The evening ended when Carmine Costanza rubbed his nose with the back of his hand. According to Maria's late mother, rubbing the nose signaled a fight. Maria always listened to her mother.

From three in the afternoon to three the following morning, Maria played not just her cards but the men who had come to "… teach her a lesson." Butch, Jimmy and Carmine attended every month. On a rotating schedule, a mayor, county commissioner, state senator, personal injury lawyer and several CEOs joined the game. They were all male, moneyed and brimming with machismo. Maria found their determination to beat her amusing. They did not. Since she was alone in the suite with these men, she kept a Glock 19 in her lap. Should the need arise, she would not hesitate to use it and, since she was a crack shot, there was a good chance that she would win that hand as well.

Vincent used his wife's poker nights to handle out of town business. He always arrived home anxious to hear Maria's account of the game and the players. Along with all her other qualities, she was an amazing and amusing storyteller.

Vincent's Movado Eliro watch was chiming four when he arrived at the Ritz Carlton. The suite was empty except for the accumulated litter tossed around by the poker players. Even over the burnt cigar stench that permeated the air, he could detect Maria's perfume. He followed the heady scent into the adjoining room, knowing that when Maria sprayed her breasts with $441.18 per ounce Annick Goutel Eau d'Hardien, it had been a good night at the tables. Vincent also knew it would be an even better night in the boudoir. He immediately forgot the pain in his back.

Anticipating the pleasure that lay ahead, Vincent kicked off his shoes and removed his tie before entering the bedroom. His suit jacket, balanced on one finger, was slung casually over his shoulder. In his other hand, he cradled two glasses of Henri IV Dudognon Heritage Cognac Grande Champagne with much- deserved reverence. Known as the DNA of Cognac, a bottle sold for $2,000,000.

Dressed in a beautiful peignoir, Maria was sitting up in bed reading when Vincent came through the door. With a suaveness few suspected he possessed, Vincent tossed his jacket onto a chair and placed the drinks on the night stand, spilling a little of the expensive liquor onto his hand. He reached for and pulled Maria from the bed, twirling her about the room while singing the Tony Bennett standard *Rags to Riches*.

"I know I'd go from rags to riches..."

"Vincent, everyone can hear you," Maria shushed him.

"... if you would only say you care."

"Are you drunk?"

"And though my pockets may be empty..." Vincent held Maria tight as he whirled around the bedroom.

Laughing, Maria removed her hand from Vincent's palm and seductively sucked the spilled cognac from his fingers. He momentarily stopped breathing, pulling Maria to him and kissing her with a fervor he rarely felt except when facing danger and the possibility of death. Maria did not close her eyes, preferring to stare back into Vincent's deep blue orbs. When the kiss ended, she trailed a hand from Vincent's face down his chest and just past his waist. With haste, he picked her up and, stumbling slightly, dropped her onto the bed. He quickly removed his shirt, belt and pants. Maria slid to the center of the mattress just as Vincent jumped onto it. Their heads collided, sending Maria into the headboard and Vincent onto the floor.

"Oh, fuck!"

"Vincent, are you all right." Maria touched the back of her head and felt for blood.

"Fuck! Fuck! Fuck!"

"Vincent, please, the other guests will hear you."

"To hell with the guests. I think I screwed up my back again. What the hell were you doing?"

"I'm sorry. I was trying to give you more room." Try as she might, Maria could not help but laugh.

"It's a king-sized bed. How much frickin' room could you need. I'm glad this amuses you, Maria. It's the last time I try to be romantic. Shit! My back!"

"I'm sorry. You're right. This isn't funny. What do you want to do?

"What do you think? Help me get up."

"All right. All right. Don't get pissy with me."

"Oh, I'm sorry. I'm lying here like a frickin' turtle with my head up my ass, and you're laughing like a hyena, but I shouldn't get pissy?"

"It is sort of funny. Where's your sense of humor?"

"I traded it in for agonizing pain."

"See, you can be funny."

"Screw you."

"I think the time for that has passed."

"Maria, I swear…"

The no-longer-loving repartee ended when a knock sounded on the door. Having received complaints of cursing and yelling from other guests, the hotel concierge was inquiring if help was needed. Maria assured him that everything was fine and wished him a "Buona notte." He left, muttering "… puttana" to himself as he sashayed down the hallway.

Marco Molina was a small man of indeterminate age… a nervous man whose constant hand gestures led observers to think "finocchio" or the more common slang "fanook." He wore thick black glasses, walked with a mincing step and spoke with a heavy Italian accent. Despite these handicaps, he carried himself with great dignity. In fact, Marco Molina had learned to use his so-called handicaps to great advantage. The fact that he was often thought to be insignificant by guests at the hotel allowed him to observe them at their most vulnerable moments. He carried a leather bound notebook in his pocket, the pages of which were covered with valuable information. He planned to use this information to secure a comfortable retirement in his home-town of Positano on southern Italy's Amalfi Coast. Many, if not most, of the pages were dedicated to Vincent and Maria Policastro.

Maria returned to Vincent and tried to help him stand up. She pulled on his arms but, due to his size and the pain he was feeling, could not lift him.

"Do you want me to call an ambulance?"

"Are you crazy? The Feds already know enough about my life and the papers would have a field day. It's bad enough that ficcansaso will spread the word all over this hotel. Fuck! Fuck! Fuck!"

"Please stop, Vincent. He's going to come back."

"Just leave me here. Go away."

"You can't sleep on the floor all night."

"I'm fine, Maria. Just give me a pillow and a blanket and go to sleep."

Reluctantly, Maria grabbed a pillow from the bed and put it under Vincent's head. She covered him with an extra blanket.

"Are you sure you're going to be okay?

Vincent pulled the cover up to his ears, ignoring her.

"Vincent?" Maria waited for an answer but Vincent remained silent. "Fine. Be a baby."

Annoyed, she left the room, turning off the lights as she went.

# CHAPTER SEVEN

*T*he investigation into the murder of attorney Gamalial Cohen was at a standstill. Having pursued every possible lead and more than a few distant possibilities, Detectives Damian Mack and Moe Di Lorenzo were growing profoundly frustrated. Three months after dragging the attorney's dead body from the lake at the Breakers West Clubhouse, they had enough information on him to produce an episode of *This Is Your Life*, but they still knew nothing about his death.

For an attorney, Gamalial Cohen's existence had been anything but staid and sedate. At 6 feet 3 inches and 278 pounds, he was a bear of a man -- so much so that the first thought people had when meeting him was "Grizzly Adams." The reference was a nod to actor Dan Haggerty, who played the real life John "Grizzly" Adams in a 1977 television series of the same name. Cohen's hair and beard were not as long and shaggy as Haggerty's had been on the show but only by a slight bit. His facial features were reminiscent of someone who had lived their life in the wild – craggy and weathered skin, rough hands, deep set eyes that glared even in death, a large nose that had met a few too many fists, numerous scars, and a mouth that seemed to be glued into a permanent frown. The bullet hole in the middle of his forehead had no connection to either Haggerty or the long deceased Adams, who had died in 1860 in a grizzly bear attack.

Guns and grizzlies had little in common except that they were both killers. Cohen would probably have stood a better chance of survival against the bear. The 125-grain bullet used by Cohen's attacker didn't require close contact and for plowing through bone and tissue with extreme force, there was nothing like a Smith and Wesson .357 magnum.

Once G had given the bullet hole in the attorney's head a cursory examination, he focused on his mouth. When first pulled from the pond, it was the mouth that had grabbed the medical examiner's attention. There was something about the way the severely chapped lips were extended, as though pouting, that seemed artificial. Upon closer inspection, G realized he wasn't looking at lips but rather a tongue protruding from between the lips. To his experienced eye, the tongue looked much too small for a man with such large features. Forcing the corpse's mouth open immediately provided the reason. The tongue wasn't Cohen's but rather one that had been severed from another body.

Damian Mack stood above the medical examiner's crouched figure, watching. "Is that a tongue?"

"It is, Detective. Based on the small size, I believe it belongs to a woman. You now have several mysteries to solve. Who killed our vic and why? Whose tongue is in his mouth and whose mouth is now home to his tongue?"

Moe Di Lorenzo joined the conversation. "I sent two uniforms to the Cohen house at The Enclave. I told them to stay outside and wait for us unless there appears to be a problem."

The Enclave was a small, exclusive neighborhood of nine large homes within Breakers West, the elegantly gated community just a few miles west of the Florida Turnpike on Okeechobee Boulevard. The development was situated on almost 700 acres of pristine nature that was a sanctuary for numerous species of birds and indigenous wildlife. Living in Breakers West was like living in an oil painting of Old Florida... towering pines, ballerina palms bending in the breeze, crystal clear lakes and manicured lawns gave homeowners the feeling that they were safe from intruders determined to destroy their fantasy world. The one-acre lot homes at The Enclave were built on a private island accessible only by a private road with enhanced security.

No sooner were the words out of Detective Di Lorenzo's mouth then Officer Keith McKinney's name appeared on his cell phone's caller I.D.

"Moe, one of the glass panels in the front door is broken. The door is open. Do you want us to enter?"

"Go in. If the wife is there, just say that her husband has been in an accident and detectives from the scene will arrive shortly. Don't answer any questions. Play dumb. That should be easy."

Before the connection was broken, the young officer could be heard saying to his partner, "Blubber guts thinks he's a comedian. I think a little payback is due."

Moe Di Lorenzo exchanged glances with Damian Mack. They both smiled. Tormenting their brothers in blue was a part of the job. Officer Keith McKinney was one of their favorite teammates. Both Moe and Mack respected his ability to assess a situation before deciding that it was necessary to fire his weapon. Many a life… criminal and cop… had been saved by McKinney's superior observation skills.

"I think you should expect some form of retaliation in the near future, Moe. Remember the last time you teased McKinney in front of his brothers. You ended up with egg on your face… literally."

Damian Mack's warning was a reference to McKinney's success at playing a practical joke on Moe a few months ago. An exploding egg sandwich had brought the department to its knees with laughter so surprised was the look on Moe's face.

"Yeah. I'll be careful. Don't want to be caught with my pants down… literally or figuratively."

After ten years with the homicide division, Detectives Di Lorenzo and Mack had developed skills of their own. They intuitively knew that something terrible was waiting for them at the Cohen house. As G drove away in the Medical Examiner's van, they set out for the family's residence. Before they even turned onto the main road, Keith McKinney called again.

"It's worse than I thought. Both the wife and kid are dead. One shot to the back of the head while sleeping. The wife... this is pretty weird... there's a tongue sticking out of her mouth and it's not hers."

Gamalial Cohen had long since stopped spending his time pacing before a judge. He no longer had an army of associates in New York, Los Angeles and Chicago. The big corner offices overlooking the Rockefeller Center skating rink and Rodeo Drive were gone as was the view of the Chicago skyline from Willis Tower. Getting his name in the paper was a thing of the past; low profile being the choice he made once he agreed to represent one client and one client only – the Policastro crime family.

As a young defense attorney, Cohen was known for his fire and brimstone tactics in the courtroom. Just the sound of his voice was enough to conjure images of the bible, thunder, lightning and burning bushes. When Cohen talked, God spoke through him... or so his grateful clients thought. When a witness was faced with cross examination by him, his questions were akin to a million paper cuts on a newborn's skin. By the time an attestant stepped out of the "iron maiden," as his associates liked to call the witness box, their reputations and credibility were bloodied.

To his enemies, who were mostly prosecutors and law enforcement officials, he was known as "Torquemada." To other defense attorneys, especially those who dreamed of emulating his brilliance in court, he was "The Grand Inquisitor." In the media, he was described both as "aggressive... an egotist on a perpetual adrenalin high" and "smooth as butter." Cohen was successful because he had the ability to think like a juror. He explained complex matters in laymen's terms that were never condescending. His demeanor was that of a father instructing his child. When other attorneys were coming unglued, Cohen appeared cool and in control... unfazed by even the most unexpected turn of events.

Above all else, he spoke with total conviction of his client's innocence even when he knew they were guilty as all hell.

Known for referencing odd bits of facts from cases long filed away in dust covered boxes; admired for his ability to recite obscure legal precedence; and both revered and reviled for remembering contradictory testimony even when under intense pressure, Gamalial Cohen was King David in the courtroom until the day he represented a captain in Vincent Policastro's army. Vitorio Anastasia's rank was of no importance when choosing to hire the high priced Cohen. Rather, the fact that he was a favorite first cousin of Maria Policastro made the decision a no brainer.

Anastasia had strangled his 28-year-old wife with a coat hanger. The case was cut and dry... a slam dunk for the prosecution. Neighbors heard Angela Anastasia screaming for her husband to "... stop, Vitorio! Stop!" He was seen running from their apartment within seconds of Angela going mute. His and Angela's fingerprints were the only ones found at the scene, and although getting a clear print from a thin piece of metal was difficult, forensic experts with the Chicago Police Department worked their magic and pulled enough of a partial to convict Vitorio. A definite slam dunk... until Gamalial Cohen showed up to speak to his new client.

Defense attorneys, by nature of their chosen profession, give creditability to the scientific concept of humans being bicameral. That's not a sexual preference. Bicameral literally means having two legislative chambers – as in two sides of the brain. Although connected, the two halves of the brain have the unique ability to function independently of each other at the same time. Each side controls specific functions and reacts differently to outside stimulus.

When addressing the jury in his opening statement, Gamalial Cohen used his most paternalistic voice to explain bicameral in simple terms. "The left brain functions include the use of logic, being detail oriented, able to form strategies, having a grasp of words and language and an awareness of order and patterns. The left side is factually ruled.

The right side of the brain controls feelings... the imagination, philosophical thinking, the ability to fantasize and see possibilities. The right side allows for impetuousness and risk taking. The right side also "believes," which can often be the source of much hubris."

Having stated his temporary insanity defense of Vitorio Anastasia to the six men and six women on the jury, Cohen set out the facts as he saw them. His client was high on caffeine at the time of the crime. Vitorio had imbibed in excess of 20 cans of high energy drinks and too many to remember cups of espresso while also taking diet pills. The combination made him mentally unstable, which led to his imagining that his wife was having an affair.

The media had a field day with the "Murder by Coffee" defense. As one reporter wrote, "The coffee/caffeine connection is unique. Jittery, I understand. Too much caffeine keeps me awake and causes me to grind my teeth, but strangulation? I usually reserve those thoughts for nights when my wife's snoring rattles the rafters."

The reporter was correct about one thing. Gamalial Cohen's strategy was, indeed, unique. In court he displayed exemplary language skills, turning what could only be described as fantastical into some-thing totally believable. He convinced the jury that his client had not intended to commit murder and was unable to form intent due to the high intake of caffeine. The verdict: not guilty of first-degree murder by reason of temporary insanity. The sentence: commitment to a mental health facility for one year or until such time as doctors deter-mined he was no longer a threat to himself and others.

The trial made Gamalial Cohen a household name around the Policastro kitchen table. His days in the public eye were over. Vincent had not become the head of one of the most powerful crime families because he did not recognize a gift horse when it was neighing right in front of him. The minute Cohen presented his case in defense of Vitorio Anastasia to the jury, Vincent knew he had found his consigliore – the man who would be his trusted advisor and confidante. It would be Cohen's job not only to represent Vincent in all business and personal matters; it would also be his job to challenge and argue with Vincent similar to the manner in which he argued in court – to ensure that all plans were foolproof. The fact that Vincent offered Cohen "more money than God" probably had a lot to do with his decision to turn his legal empire over to his partners.

In death, Gamalial Cohen would be facing the biggest case of his life. Having more money than God did not guarantee entry to a blissful afterlife. In fact, with God as the ultimate judge and jury, it was anyone's guess whether Cohen's earthly wealth and power would have a negative or positive effect on the direction his soul would travel.

# CHAPTER EIGHT

*D*espite a hectic schedule that left barely a minute for themselves and their families, Cat and Marci never turned down an opportunity to speak about the merits of self-preservation, especially in the form of taking responsibility for one's actions. This imperative was voiced loud and clear at every women's group and networking forum they attended. The message was not always welcomed by women who believed that the rapist should shoulder full responsibility for his actions. While Cat and Marci did not disagree about the placement of blame, they did try to drive home that fewer rapes would be committed if more women were vigilant about the need to protect themselves and if rape was given its just status as a violent crime rather than being classified as a sex crime.

One topic kept surfacing at these meetings, with the attendees being equally divided on the proper course of action. The U.S. Supreme Court was reviewing the legitimacy of life sentences without the possibility of parole for juveniles who committed criminal acts that did not result in murder. There were currently 129 prisoners under the age of eighteen serving life terms for such crimes—77 of those convictions in Florida. Cat and Marci tried to explain how the inability to sentence teenage rapists to life in prison could be detrimental to society.

"Recently, our esteemed justices…," Cat began, "… in a split decision, ruled that criminals such as Nathan Walker and Jakaris Taylor could possibly roam free to prey upon the innocent once again. You may recall from news reports that Walker was 16 and Taylor was 15 in 2007 when they, along with other gang members, tortured and repeatedly raped a 35-year-old women, eventually forcing her to have sex with her 12-year-old son, who they had also beaten. The facts of this case are so horrendous that revisiting them even for this discussion is painful, but I will as the only way to make an informed decision is to know everything that happened. What I am going to read to you has been taken from a recent newspaper account of the attack.

'On the 18th of June in 2007, at nine in the evening, a 35-year-old woman came home to her apartment in the Dunbar Village housing project in West Palm Beach, Florida. She had just finished up a long day of delivering telephone books and she was tired. While making dinner for herself and her son, there was a knock at the door.

A young black male told her that her truck had a flat tire and that she should come outside to take a look. Following the apparent good Samaritan outside, she hadn't taken more than a few steps when three teenagers—all wearing masks and all carrying guns—pointed the weapons at her and told her to get back into her apartment.

They hit her, knocking her to the floor. They pushed her son down to the floor as well. They demanded money, which she didn't have. Incensed, the four boys beat the woman and her son, stripped the woman of her clothing, took her to the bedroom and raped her over and over, with each boy taking his turn. Her son was held at gunpoint and forced to watch as they raped and sodomized her. She cried out in pain and fear, but nobody came to help, not then, not when she heard her son cry out as they stripped him naked as well, sporadically breaking light bulbs and plates on his head.

Up to five other teenagers arrived, but they came to join in the cruelty—not to help the victims. These boys also raped and sodomized the woman, recording it on a cell phone. Then, holding a gun to the 12-year-old's head, the gang forced the woman to perform oral sex on her son.

Eventually, they forced mother and son into the bathtub, which they filled with vinegar and water. They poured common household cleaning products over her, including hydrogen peroxide, rubbing alcohol, nail polish remover and an ammonia based cleaning product. Ammonia was also thrown into her son's eyes. One of the gang forced a bar of soap into the woman's vagina, hoping to remove physical evidence. Someone suggested setting the mother and her son on fire. Not finding a lighter, they left with the warning that if they got out of the tub, they would be killed. Thirty minutes later, while the mother and her son were still in the tub, one of the teenagers returned to sexually assault the woman again.

Mother and son stayed in the apartment for two hours after the attack. Nobody came to investigate their screams, nobody called the police for help. Because their assailants had stolen their cell phone, their home phone and their fax machine, they were unable to call for assistance. It was a long walk to the Good Samaritan Medical Center, but they walked the mile together.

Both mother and son were badly injured. The boy had to be immobilized for more than two days on his hospital bed, with bandages covering both eyes and a two-inch gash on the top of his skull.'

It took two years for the case to go to trial. Two years of having to relive that night over and over again -- depositions, statements to the police, appointments with therapists – all the while fearing retribution from friends of the assailants. Tommy Poindexter, Nathan Walker Jr. and Jakaris Taylor were sentenced to life in prison without parole. At the sentencing hearing, the victim's attorney read a letter to the court describing her life since the attack. Her heart-wrenching words portrayed the terror that constantly followed mother and son. Friends of the defendants laughed as her letter was read.

If, while still too young to vote or drink, these boys could perpetrate such heinous acts on other human beings, I must ask, 'Would you want them back on the streets in a few years?'

Cat sat down and Marci continued the discussion.

"The life sentence of Milagro Cunningham is also in question. He was 15 when he kidnapped an eight-year-old Lake Worth girl, raped and beat her and then disposed of her body like it was nothing more than a rag doll. To hide his crime, he took that little girl, still alive, to a deserted landfill, where he threw her into a recycling bin and covered her with a pile of rocks. Cunningham left her to die -- but she didn't. By some miracle, she was found and survived her injuries.

The decision of the Supreme Court that a sentence of life without parole in crimes where death does not occur violates the constitutional guarantee against cruel and unusual punishment is, to me, absurd. I have seen hundreds of victims of violent crimes, and I can tell you with absolute certainty that death takes many forms. The survivors of violent crimes suffer death anew every day for the rest of their lives. Unfortunately, the rights of the victim continue to be less important than the rights of the criminal. The justices believe that, regardless of the heinous nature of their actions, juveniles should be given a chance to prove that they have been rehabilitated. Allow me to read from Justice Kennedy's brief:

'Those who commit truly horrifying crimes as juveniles may turn out to be irredeemable, and thus deserving of incarceration for the duration of their lives. But the Eighth Amendment does forbid states from making the judgment at the outset that these offenders never will be fit to reenter society.'

We must ask ourselves what motivates a child to commit crimes of abuse and torture. If someone willingly abases another human being to a level below animal, was that individual ever fit to live in society? Is there any reason to waste the court's time and citizens' money revisiting the possibility of parole when we already know what the result of freedom will be?

Florida has the severest sentencing rate of any state in the country.

In recent years, Palm Beach County has seen a rise in brutal crimes perpetrated against the innocent and unprotected. The courts have dealt with those criminals in the harshest of terms -- as they should. Now, thanks to the Supreme Court's ruling, each of these cases must be revisited and the sentences re-examined.

Anytime a deadly weapon is part of the equation, the life without parole guideline should not be off the table... no matter the age of the perpetrator. To an eight-year-old, the hands and fists of a 15- year-old are a deadly weapon as is every part of his anatomy. Additionally, if someone is old enough to load and point a gun, he is old enough to suffer the consequences for firing said gun or even for just pointing it at his victim.

On November 15, 2009, the opinion page of the Palm Beach Post featured commentary by then Florida Assistant Attorney General John Bajger. Titled *If crime isn't murder, life without parole is too much*, Mr. Bajger devoted a large portion of his writing to describing some of the juveniles serving life sentences. He briefly touched on their crimes but never gave specific details. At the time, I found it morally reprehensible that he devoted a mere three sentences to the Dunbar Village attack.

Mr. Bajger wrote that 'By focusing on punishment alone, the system is blind to factors that should mitigate juvenile sentences.' He also claimed that such sentencing '... contains a disturbing racial aspect.'

As a law enforcement officer and as a conscientious citizen, I resent when the race card is thrown into rational discussion. Are there more minority offenders in Florida prisons? Probably. Do they commit a large percentage of the crimes? I don't have exact figures, but based on the population and the statistics available, I would have to say yes. Does my favoring a life sentence make me a racist? No. A criminal's skin color is unimportant to me. I want *all* criminals punished and removed from the streets so that good people, regardless of their ethnicity, are protected.

Mr. Bajger further stated that 'As a civilized society that believes in the sanctity of all human life, we cannot permit our criminal justice system to throw away the lives of juveniles as irretrievably bad.'

Think back over the details of the Dunbar Village case which my partner just read to you and tell me if the men who committed those crimes displayed any sense of sanctity for human life. Yes, I did say men... not boys.

In 2009, State Rep. William Snyder explained it very succinctly. 'At a certain point, juveniles cross the line, and they have to be treated as adults and punished as adults.'

I have often heard people claim the nurture versus nature argument in defending their position against the *without parole* stipulation. Pain is something we learn at a very early age; perhaps, from the very moment of birth. Maybe, even, before birth. We've all felt it. We all know it isn't pleasant. Thus, if we know pain and we do not want to suffer pain, why do some willingly inflict it on others?

The men involved in the Dunbar Village attack perpetrated unspeakable cruelties on their victims. They could have stopped; walked away at any time. Rather, they discussed what further tortures they could inflict. They were not coerced or threatened. They made a conscious decision to continue their heinous actions.

There comes a time when we must recognize that just because we are human does not mean we are humane. Those who have forsaken humanity, no matter their age, should wait for final judgment in prison where they can't hurt anyone else.

Palm Beach County Judge Krista Marx had the thankless job of re-sentencing the men involved in the Dunbar Village case as well as others guilty of horrific acts of violence. Attorneys doubt that what they deem her *harsh* sentencing of 60 years will hold up on appeal. Harsh? Harsh is what happens to rape victims. Harsh is a woman being forced to bear unspeakable pain and never having the luxury to forget. A *harsh* sixty years is a mere slap on the wrist for these criminals."

Cat returned to the podium.

"I would like to close with my statement to the judge at the sentencing hearing for my attacker. Please keep these words in mind if you are ever called for jury duty in an assault case.

'To the court, this case is a sexual assault but to me, it is a homicide. Robert Bridgeman effectively used the machete he carried to take away a part of my life. I am no longer the person I used to be, and I doubt that time will bring back the old me. If I have to suffer physical and emotional pain for the rest of my life, then Mr. Bridgeman should have to pay with the rest of his life. He should not be allowed an opportunity to victimize another woman.'

No one -- no man, woman or child -- should ever have to fear that their attacker, no matter that attacker's age, will one day be free to finish the job he or she started. Robert Bridgeman did not kill me the day he raped me. Rather, he returned weeks later and hid in the shadows, waiting for an opportunity to finish what he had started the morning he pressed the blade of a machete against my throat." Cat unbuttoned the top of her blouse and bent her head back to reveal the deep two-inch scar on her neck.

"By the grace of God, I am standing here before you and he has taken up permanent residence in a graveyard. Few people are as lucky as I was."

~

"Do you think anyone really hears our message, Cat? Do you think those women were really listening?"

Cat and Marci always left these speaking engagements filled with mixed emotions. They were happy to be able to spread their warning to "… stay safe." They were equally concerned that far too many women embraced the "It won't happen to me" mindset until it did happen to them, and then it was too late.

"I don't know, Marci. We can only hope that, should they ever be in danger, they will remember what we've said. If even one woman is spared the trauma of rape, then all I went through will be worth it."

"To quote Sherlock Holmes, 'I confess that I have been blind as a mole, but it is better to learn wisdom late than never to learn it at all.'"

"Sir Arthur was a masterful writer. Sometimes I think he was writing specifically for us, Marci."

Cat was just about to slide into the passenger seat of their car when she noticed writing on the window. The writing was faint... written with what appeared to be bar soap. At first, the words seemed to make no sense, but Cat quickly realized they were part of a message which began on the front windshield.

"Marci, do you see what I see?"

Marci was already following the writing on the driver's window around to the front of the car.

"It begins here. 'Buried deep below the ground. Two with a head-stone. Two unfound. Death is waiting all around.'" Marci had walked her way around the car and was now standing next to Cat. "He's not much of a poet."

"He who? Is writing ability all you're worried about? This is a threat to my life. Either someone wants revenge for Bobby Bridge-man's death or there's a copycat killer waiting to strike."

"Cat, read the poem again. Read it aloud. Who does it sound like? You've read something like this before."

"When?"

"Read it."

"Buried deep below the ground. Two with headstones. Two unfou... Shit! It sounds like the poem Brandon Hanson sent to his teacher."

"Yes, it does. I don't know if Hanson is toying with you or is actu-ally a threat, but we now have a proof that his innocent face hides a devious mind."

"Obviously, he is not traveling as his mother would like us to believe. Let's find him and nail his ass to the wall."

"Deal. Now, let's get the car back to the compound before it rains."

# CHAPTER NINE

*M*aria Policastro shut the bedroom light and gently closed the door behind her. She made her way across the litter strewn floor of the living room by the moonlight shining in through the wall-sized window. Exhausted, she dropped her right hip onto the sofa and pulled her knees to her chest. She was still in the fetal position when housekeeping knocked on the door at 1:00 in the afternoon.

Groggy and aching from the cramped posture her body had held for the last eight hours, she stumbled to the main door of the suite to let in the cleaning crew. There was no need to apologize for the condition of the room; these same three women were paid handsomely every month to repair and replace what the poker players had damaged or destroyed and to repeat as often as necessary, "Me no comprende ingles." With her eyes still half closed, Maria turned and walked toward the bedroom. Ear to the door, she heard no sounds… no snoring, no groaning, no cursing. She assumed Vincent had fallen into a much needed deep sleep and was still in dreamland.

Turning the doorknob slowly so as not to wake her husband, Maria made her way toward the bathroom. A hot shower would ease her aching muscles and wash the cigar smoke and ashes from her body and hair. The sun's rays were penetrating the heavy drapes and shining directly onto Vincent's face as she crossed the room. That's when Maria became fully conscious. Her scream should have woken the dead, but it had no effect on Vincent.

Hearing Maria's frantic pleas for Vincent to "... wake up," the cleaning crew called the hotel manager who then called the Sheriff's Office. Homicide Detectives Cat Leigh and Marci Welles were on duty. Along with Damian Mack and Moe Di Lorenzo, they arrived at the Ritz Carlton within 20 minutes of getting word that organized crime boss Vincent Policastro was dead. Medical Examiner Dr. Mark Geschwer was right behind them.

Normally, only one team of detectives was sent to the scene of a homicide, but Vincent Policastro's death following so closely on the heels of Gamalial Cohen's murder required special attention. Since Mack and Moe were already assigned to the Cohen case, they tagged along to see if the two deaths were related... not that they doubted they were even for a second.

Emotionally, Maria Policastro was the most in control recent widow Cat and Marci had ever interviewed. Considering that she had found her husband's body just 90 minutes earlier, she was amazingly reserved. The fact that Vincent had been shot through the temple at close range when she was only 50 feet away did not seem to faze her one bit. Her dry eyes, steady hands and calm exterior expressed a level of detachment far beyond any the detectives had seen so far in their careers.

Putting her storytelling skills to good use, Maria detailed for Cat and Marci how Vincent had arrived at the hotel feeling more amorous than usual.

"When Vincent entered the bedroom, he was already barefoot. His suit jacket hung over his shoulder hooked on one finger. He was carrying two glasses of cognac and looked like a movie star. He was singing *Rags to Riches*. That was his favorite Tony Bennett song; he considered it something of a personal anthem. Vincent's voice... it's the type best used in the shower with the water running full force but he was having so much fun putting on a show for me, I couldn't help but laugh. It was good to see him happy.

Since Vincent is... was... rarely so animated, I assumed that his New York trip had been a success. He had a bad back so when he pulled me from the bed and began dancing around the room, I was surprised. His palms were sticky with spilled cognac. I put his fingers in my mouth and sucked on them. Then, I ran my hand over his face, down his chest and... lower... I began to loosen his belt. Vincent picked me up and tossed me onto the bed. He undressed quickly."

Right about this time, Marci began to nibble on her cuticles. Cuticle biting was a habit she had been trying to break for years and, until tonight, had been fairly successful. She had even gotten a French manicure for Cat's wedding... a true sign of how deeply she valued their friendship.

Since Cat's brutal beating and rape in 2007, Marci had stayed away from nail salons. The odor of polish remover and camphor had the same effect on her that garlic had on Dracula... sheer terror. The sights, sounds and smells of anything manicure related reminded her that the wonderful girls' day out they had shared -- a day which had included mani-pedis -- had ended with Cat looking like the Elephant Man.

Both G and Cat had sighed with relief when Marci finally broke the cuticle biting habit. They had grown weary of warning her of the health issues that dead bodies posed, especially should the seepage from a corpse get into her mouth. Gloves were no guarantee of protection. Unfortunately, it had been the stress of solving murders that had driven Marci to bite the skin from her fingers in the first place.

Today, Vincent Policastro's death came close to undoing all the good that had been done. Any time someone insisted on giving graphic descriptions of their sex life, Marci had to physically restrain herself from chomping on her finger tips like a beaver with a log. She wasn't a prude; she just didn't want to hear the juicy stuff unless said juice was directly related to her case.

Fearing that any interruption of Maria's narrative would result in missing an important clue, Cat and Marci listened carefully. When Maria got to the part about smashing their heads together after Vincent pounced on the bed like a jaguar, she smiled as if the memory was a pleasant one. She even asked the detectives if they wanted to feel the bump on the back of her skull. Finally, she told them about Vincent's petulant behavior, his decision to sleep on the floor and her decision to sleep in the living room. She said she had slept soundly until the maids awakened her sometime after noon. That's when she re-entered the bedroom and found Vincent dead.

"Can you think of anyone who would want to kill your husband, Mrs. Policastro?"

"Seriously, Detective Leigh? It would be easier to tell you who didn't want to kill him, and I would probably be the only name on the list."

"All of his subordinates… they all had a reason to end his life?"

"Many reasons, but reasons to kill him and actually killing him are two different things. Every wife has a reason to kill her husband. Most don't ever do it. It was the same for Vincent's men. They didn't always like the decisions he made because often those decisions cost them money, but they abided by them. Now, his business associates... that's another group entirely. I know little about them so the person you must speak with is Ernie Mastrianno. He was Vincent's right hand on all company matters."

"What company would that be?"

"Vincent had many business interests but his primary one was Crotone Moving Company in Boynton Beach."

"We'll need you to give us a list of everyone… friend and foe… who you consider possible suspects."

"For that information, you will need to speak to Ernie. You'll find him at the Crotone offices between 8 am and 5 pm. After that, you can visit him at The Firehouse strip club. He's usually there until he kicks the last pervert out sometime around 2 am."

"You said your husband hurt his back. Was he seeing a doctor?" Now that all discussion of sex was over, Marci felt comfortable joining the interrogation.

"Why, yes, Detective Welles, he was. His name is Michael Vitale."

"Where can we find him?"

"In the phone book."

~

"I think we should discuss this case with your father, Cat. His insights could be invaluable." Marci was making notes in pad while Cat drove them back to the station after their less than fruitful meeting with Maria Policastro.

"Marci, my dad is retired. He hasn't had any contact with his former patients in a long time, and even if he did, I wouldn't put him in that kind of danger."

"I didn't say he should reveal top secret information. I just thought he could ask... you know, conversationally... if Blackie knew Vincent Policastro."

"No. Anyway, Blackie is retired and my father has no contact with him."

"Crooks retire?"

"Wealthy ones do. Blackie moved to Las Vegas many years ago. He spends his days playing poker... winning and losing fortunes on the turn of a card. My dad has no contact with him."

"Well, it was worth a shot. Hey, I made a joke!" Marci laughed at the unintentional pun.

Cat just stared at the road ahead and hoped that the conversation was over.

# CHAPTER TEN

inding Ernie Mastrianno was easy. With Vincent dead, he was busy keeping Crotone Moving on schedule. Little of that schedule actually had to do with moving furniture. The primary cargo was money derived from gambling and drugs. Sometimes stolen cars were a part of the transport and sometimes the owners of those cars were also moved... usually deep into the Everglades where no one would find them.

Ernie was very good at moving women as well, but their movements had nothing to do with locations and everything to do with gyrations. He was co-owner and manager of The Firehouse, a strip club with a high opinion of itself. The sign over the door read *Gentlemen's Club*. In his early 60s, Ernie was a clone of his late boss only in a cheaper, less well-made suit. He had a full head of white hair, a nose that bent at several different angles and eyes that never missed a trick. Like Maria, he was a keen observer of human behavior, and Maria hated him for it.

When Cat and Marci entered the office at Crotone Moving, Ernie stood and moved around the desk to greet them. He held the backs of two chairs as though waiting for royalty to be seated. Cat and Marci remained standing. Ernie understood the maneuver. He used it himself when he wanted to intimidate someone. Standing was power. Sitting was a sign of weakness.

"The friendship between me and Vincent goes back 50 years. It began in the third grade of St. Peter and Paul Grammar School in Hoboken, New Jersey. On the first day of classes, we recognized the prankster in each other and began spending our after school hours together. Most of the time we amused ourselves by making phone calls and asking homeowners if their refrigerators were running or if they had Prince Philip in a can. If a homeowner answered 'Yes' to either of those questions, we laughingly told them to '... catch it before it got away' or '... let him out before he suffocates.' It was innocent kid stuff."

Marci and Cat knew a fish story when they heard one. They had done their homework before meeting Ernie Mastrianno face to face. While there was no denying that the two men had been kids sometime in the past, innocence was a quality that neither could list on their resume. As Vincent and Ernie got older, their so-called pranks became more serious, progressing from petty theft and pick pocketing to home invasions and robbery. Murder was still a far way off.

With great humor, Ernie told Cat and Marci and that he and Vincent were "... natural athletes with a special interest in track and field. We didn't need no practice field. We trained on the streets of Hoboken."

Again, because they had done their due diligence, Cat and Marci knew that the training Ernie referenced was running away from the law. Dodging arrest had proven to be effective exercise. By some twist of fate, neither Ernie nor Vincent ever did a minute of jail time while they were juveniles.

Contrary to the popular belief that criminals are stupid, both men graduated high school at the top of their class. Vincent went to college and earned a business degree. Ernie went straight to work. His first job was procuring girls for The Booby Trap, a strip club in Jersey City, New Jersey. After a year he became manager of that club and when

Vincent graduated college, they bought the club from the owner, who did not want to sell. Encouragement was found at the ends of Ernie's and Vincent's arms in the form of hard hitting fists. They renamed the club The Firehouse and painted the front door red. Inside, there was an oversized brass bell on the back wall near the entrance to the private rooms. Whenever a man got lucky, he rang it. The poles on the stage in the center of the main room needed no explanation. Ten years ago, they "bought" another club—this one in West Palm Beach—and named it The Firehouse Too.

During their long partnership, Vincent served as the idea man while Ernie was the numbers guy. Vincent trusted him to handle the financial end of all their ventures, including collecting overdue debts from delinquent loan recipients. Ernie no longer used his fists, preferring to allow his protégés to hone their skills under his excellent tutelage. In the inner city neighborhoods of Hudson County, New Jersey, and any city in south Florida from Tequesta to Boca Raton, it was not unusual for hospitals to see an increase in business at the end of each month. Broken jaws, arms, ribs, legs… broken bones of every sort were the most common reason for people to visit the emergency room.

Since Vincent had a vested interest in The Firehouse, Cat and Marci made the strip club a stop in their quest for answers. Immediately upon entering, they realized that the strip club was not your run of the mill pole vaulting business. This particular den of iniquity combined truly beautiful women with gourmet food that often earned five stars in the restaurant review section of the Palm Beach Post. Almost 70% of the patrons were males between the ages of 21 and 50. The remaining 30% were women between 25 and "You look great for your age." When Cat and Marci arrived a little after three in the afternoon, business was booming.

The first person to approach the detectives was Jeannetta Jordan, the house manager and sometimes waitress. Despite the bleached blonde hair, heavy makeup and dark circles under her eyes, she could have passed for much younger than her 35 years… her birth date clearly visible on the driver's license she held out as a form of identification. Jeannetta, who intentionally exaggerated the pronunciation of her name… "It sounds like two words – Jean Netta. I was named for my Grandma Jean and my Grandma Annetta," she told Cat and Marci when she introduced herself.

Word had already spread to the club that Vincent was dead. No doubt Ernie Mastrianno had given special orders to his employees on what they could and could not say to the cops. Jeannetta led Cat and Marci to a table near a window in the dining room area of the club.

"Can I get you something to eat or drink, Detectives?"

"No, thanks. We just have some questions we'd like you to answer." Marci looked around the restaurant, impressed by the somewhat subdued décor. If not for the excess of mammaries and thighs, she might actually be fooled into thinking this was a class joint.

"How well did you know Vincent Policastro?"

"Not really well… not in a personal sense. Ernie runs the club. Mr. Vince came in from time to time when he needed… when he needed a massage."

"You have masseurs on staff?" Cat had all she could do to keep from laughing out loud.

The questioning look in Jeannetta's eyes was a clear signal that the word *masseur* was foreign to her. Cat rephrased her question.

"Do you have professional massage therapists on staff?"

"I guess that depends on what you mean by professional and what kind of massage you're looking for." Jeannetta smiled with faux innocence.

Marci's dislike for overt sexuality was causing her to clench her fists. She was determined not to put her fingers in her mouth in front of Jeannetta.

"Just tell us what you know about Vincent Policastro."

"Well, he liked banana pancakes for breakfast and lots of hot, fresh coffee. No decaf. He liked the high octane kind of java. He always ordered sausages, home fries and rye toast, butter on the side."

It was Cat's turn to look confused. "I didn't know you served breakfast here."

"We don't. I also work the early morning shift at the Ritz Carlton."

"What does that have to do with Vincent Policastro?"

"Mr. Vince and Mrs. Policastro are guests at the hotel at least once a month. The first time he saw me there, he didn't make the connection between my working at the club and being a waitress at the hotel."

"And after he made the connection... what happened then?"

"I remember the day I worked two shifts – first at the Ritz and then later in the day here. Mr. Vince was sitting at the bar having a drink. This was when I was still riding the poles. I could feel him staring at me. He bent over and whispered into Ernie's ear, and Ernie started laughing. He was laughing really hard and Mr. Vince looked annoyed."

"Why do you think that was?"

"I got the feeling Mr. Vince wasn't too happy that the broad rubbing her butt against the pole might have touched his eggs and bacon.

Anyway, Ernie must have told Mr. Vince about my morning job because while I was taking a cigarette break in the back alley, Mr. Vince came outside. He said, 'You're a good dancer. I hear you have a little girl and nobody to help with expenses.' With that, he hands me a wad of bills – a thousand dollars when I counted it – and told me to take the rest of the day off. He was a nice man."

"Heartwarming." Marci wasn't interested in any feel good stories about a cold blooded killer. "Can you remember anything unusual that happened here in the club... any reason why someone would want to kill him?"

"Well, there was this one day... I brought the mail to Ernie. There was a special delivery letter from the insurance company.

Ernie was furious when he opened it. He said that they were raising his rates again... second time that year... and he was beginning to think it would be better to just torch the place."

"Why would that be a reason for someone to kill Vincent?"

"Oh, it wasn't. I remember that because it was the same day the Feds showed up. They came in like gangbusters. Told all the dancers to get off the stage. Vince and Ernie were upstairs having a meeting. Ernie yelled down to us girls that we should stay where we were. There was a lot of cursing back and forth. One of the agents had a search warrant and another had an arrest warrant."

"Arrest warrant for who?" Cat was enjoying this little story even if it was taking a circuitous route to get to The End."

"For Ernie. He was supposed to be on house arrest. Don't ask me what for. Anyway, he was supposed to be wearing an ankle monitor, but he bought his mother a beautiful diamond bracelet so that she would stay at his house and wear it while he went to work."

"A mother's love is a wonderful thing." Marci smiled sardonically at Jeannetta.

"I guess it doesn't matter how old a girl happens to be... diamonds are always her best friend. Anyway, the Feds figured it out. Ernie said the warrants were payback for yanking their short hairs." Jeannetta yawned her indifference at Cat and Marci.

"What happened then?"

"The guy in charge put Ernie in hand cuffs and told him to sit at one of the downstairs tables. Another Fed watched him. The rest of them started searching the club, but it didn't really look like they were searching very hard. A few of them went back to the office. The main guy, too. They were gone the longest but when they came out, they didn't have anything in their hands... no papers, no computer... nothing. While everyone was kept occupied, Frankie—he's one of Vince's guys—got Vincent out the back before he was seen. Eventually, the Feds left taking Ernie with them. He yelled for me to lock up when the night was over."

"And you have no idea what went on in the office or where they took Ernie?"

"Well, I'm pretty sure they weren't really looking for anything. Ernie would never be stupid enough to leave incriminating evidence at the club. More than likely, they were leaving things... ears... bugs, if you know what I mean. Similar things have happened over the years and Ernie always does a sweep after the Feds leave."

"Who did the sweep this time?"

"JoJo. He's Frankie's partner. After the Feds left, he went around and found all the bugs and got rid of them. Well, he got rid of almost all of them." Jeannetta started laughing at what appeared to be a private joke.

"Something funny?" Cat asked.

"Sorry. JoJo likes to play pranks on people. He left a bug in the bathroom in Ernie's office. Then, he told the bartender to '... take a long shit...' and read Shakespeare while sitting on the can. JoJo's pretty funny, but the bartender was funnier. We could hear him in the toilet reciting Romeo and Juliet at the top of his lungs."

Driving back to the precinct, Cat and Marci went over the events of the day. Cat reviewed her notes on Jeannetta Jordan with wry amusement.

"For a waitress slash pole dancer slash restaurant manager, Ms. Jeannetta Jordan appears to have a pretty clear idea of what is happening behind the scenes. We need to take a deeper look at her life."

"She was rather savvy for someone who is only doing this job to pay the bills and care for her kid. I think she knows a lot more about what Ernie and Vincent were up to than she is letting on. Let's see what we can find out from our contacts at the FBI."

"You make the call when we get back. I'll write up our report and give a verbal to the Captain."

"What about G?"

"I'll call G and get an update on the autopsies."

"Then what?"

"We go home. I'm tired and hungry and Kevin is barbecuing steaks. It's been a long three weeks. Tomorrow, let's pay a visit to Dr. Michael Vitale, orthopedist to the mob."

"Deal."

"Shit. One of us has to call Moe and Mack. We need to compare notes. Our cases are aligned and they may have information we need."

"I'll call them in the morning if you bring me a doggie bag for lunch. Cold steak sounds great. We're having tuna casserole."

# CHAPTER ELEVEN

"*D*amn, I feel good this morning. I slept like a baby... first time in a long time." Cat stretched her arms above her head and rolled her shoulders just like a contented feline.

"The deepest sleep is found when lying next to someone you love."

"That's beautiful. I'm guessing it's not a Sherlock Holmes quote. Who said it?"

"Me!" Marci smiled broadly, proud that Cat had recognized her poetic abilities. "As much as I admire Sir Arthur's skills as a writer, he wasn't much for romance."

"You never cease to amaze me, Marci. You are an intrepid detective, much like Sherlock Holmes, and a poetess on a par with Emily Dickinson."

No sooner was the word "poetess" out of her mouth than Cat's face turned a whiter shade of pale. Despite hours upon hours of searching digital and hard paper data bases, nothing could be found linking Brandon Hanson or anyone else to the poem found on Cat's and Marci's unmarked car. When contacted shortly after the Ribbon Killer verse was discovered, Hanson's mother assured Cat and Marci that her son was not – had not been – in Florida for many weeks. From Philadelphia, he had traveled to Las Vegas and then on to California, where he was attending a writer's conference. He called her every night and the area code from which he called was 805 – Santa Barbara.

A call to the conference confirmed that Hanson was registered but no one could say whether he was actually in attendance. He had paid the registration fee. That was all that mattered.

When asked where her son was staying, his mother told the detectives that Brandon was not one for wasting money on lodging. He would cajole total strangers into letting him share a hotel room or, if they lived locally, use their couch. She was accustomed to his wandering ways and had stopped worrying about him years ago.

"He's a grown man, Detectives. I let go of the leash when he was 16. I'm happy to see him when he comes home. I'm just as happy to see him go when he leaves."

"Poetry must run in the family," Cat said to Marci as they left the Hanson household. "That '… happy to see him come/happy to see him go' line sounded like something from a rap song I once heard."

"Just wait til you hear the rap song I'm composing." Marci's laugh was full and throaty. Her dislike for rap music was well known by her partner and best friend. Forced to listen to even a few bars of a song, she would grit her teeth and mutter, "Rap! Crap!"

"Hold that thought." Cat brought the conversation back to their case, "I had an interesting conversation with Captain Constantine before going home last night. She knows our Dr. Vitale quite well… not socially… criminally. He's been on her radar for some time now. They actually met at a Race for the Cure dinner where he was honored for making a six zeros donation to support breast cancer research."

"That's a lot of broken bones that needed setting."

"You have no idea just how right you are. According to the Captain, Michael Vitale and the Policastro's went to high school together, and they are linked by more than a love for their alma mater. Vitale's name has come up in quite a number of suspicious auto accidents where the injured parties have been known to work for or been customers of Crotone Moving."

"How many car crashes does it take to make a case?"

"It's not the number. It's the lack of substantiated evidence. These are well-planned staged crashes with every detail accounted for. I spoke to Pete Shonto in Strategic Operations. By the way, he said to give you his best and tell you that the twins are now three-year-old terrors. Double the pleasure. Double the fun. And double the work."

"It was a loss when he decided to transfer out of the department, but it was the right decision for him."

Marci smiled thinking back over the five years that Moe and Pete had been partners. They cleared a lot of cases together, but Pete had never liked the daily depravity whereas Moe was a cadaver dog. He belonged in homicide, and he and Mack made a great team. Marci was glad Moe had chosen to stay with the department.

"You're right," Cat agreed. "Anyway, Pete was telling me about this thing they call a T-bone accident. The scam artist waits for an unsuspecting driver to proceed through an intersection. Just as the motorist reaches the middle, the perp hits the gas pedal and slams into the driver's door. When the police arrive, "shady helpers" – that's what they call phony witnesses – give statements claiming that the driver ran a stop sign or red light. The driver, who is stunned and shaken, denies that he was at fault but since there are witnesses…

The result is that motorist is on the hook for injuries he didn't cause. The so-called victims file personal injury claims for whiplash or soft tissue damage both of which are hard to detect. Sometimes, they even break a bone – on purpose mind you – and then they require an orthopedist."

"And I'm guessing Dr. Michael Vitale is their bone setter of choice."

"Like I said… you are an intrepid detective."

"Well, let's go see if we can T-bone some answers out of him. We've been known to pull a few scams of our own."

**Six months earlier:**

Monday nights were slow nights for the Policastro family. Usually, the evenings were reserved for counting the revenues that had been earned during the previous week. This was especially true during football and basketball season, when bets were made, paid and, for those on the losing end, collected with or without interest depending on whether they could ante up what they owed or not. Those who could not pay their debts would often spend the wee hours of Tuesday mornings in the emergency room or, at the very least, bedridden with bags of frozen peas on their broken noses. Should rhinoplasty be required to reset a shattered proboscis, Dr. Vitale's business card was tucked into the pocket of the delinquent debtor.

With his men out on the streets making their rounds, Vincent was holding court in the private dining room of the Flagler Steakhouse located at The Breakers Hotel. With him were Ernie, Frankie, JoJo, Michael Vitale and Vitale's attorney, Marvin Manker. Manker was a big man from the top of his 6 foot 9 inch - 355 pound frame to the tip of his size 13 shoes. His face resembled one of the centuries old gargoyles which stared down from the parapets of Notre Dame. Vitale, on the other hand, was a mere 6 foot 3 inches and a buff 190 pounds. He was very handsome with dark, wavy hair and a perfectly chiseled chin. While physically they were polar opposites, mentally the two men shared an aptitude for making money in unconventional ways and neither liked to be told "It can't be done."

Once the handshakes and introductions were over, Vincent set about making his guests comfortable.

"Who wants what to drink? How about a little grappa? My grandfather used to distill the stuff in the basement of his house. He gave it away for free. Now, restaurants charge $18.00 for a thimble-sized glass. Cretino..." Vincent kicked the chair where JoJo was sitting, "... go get us a double round. I don't want any servers coming in here just yet."

"You got to stop calling him that," Ernie advised Vincent as JoJo slumped towards the bar, shoulders hunched with anger. "You make him sound like an idiot."

"Well, if the shoe fits... and, in his case, it fits perfectly." Vincent turned to Michael Vitale and slapped him on the back. "So, old friend, what are these great plans you mentioned?"

"I can only speak in hypotheticals at the moment. Let's say that there is an ice cube on the floor as we leave here tonight."

"Let's say that's an accident waiting to happen."

"Exactly. You slip, fall and hurt your back. Maybe, dislocate a shoulder. You come to my office."

"I don't go to the hospital?"

"No need. I'll examine you and recommend a course of treatment. I will also suggest you see another specialist... a chiropractor."

"I don't like chiropractors. The sound of my bones cracking in my ears gives me the creeps."

"You don't have to like him, Vincent, you just have to trust him. The chiropractor will run additional tests and recommend adjustments and modalities..."

"What the fuck are modalities? I don't want any shots."

"Ultrasound... maybe massage therapy... nothing that hurts. The Chiro will recommend that you come in three times a week for a few months. As you begin to feel better, you go less often until you hit a total of 50 visits. Then, you hire Marvin as your attorney and sue."

"What would I be looking at for me?"

"Your medical bills could reach $20,000. Marvin will settle out of court for five times that amount. He takes 25%. You get 75%. Tax free."

"What about you and the bone crusher?"

"We get paid by your insurance."

"That's great, but I gotta come in three times a week and go for all those modality things."

"Who says?" Michael Vitale's forehead is creased with an expression of feigned confusion.

"You just said..." Vincent looks at his long time friend and suddenly understands why he is smirking.

"Shit! That's good. Just add a few shots to the list. I'm not going to get them anyway." Vincent laughed.

"As I said, 'You just have to trust him.'"

"And you think we can get away with this?"

"I wouldn't suggest you do it if I didn't know it was safe and there was money to be made. However, you have to do exactly what I tell you to do. First, decide which of you is going to be the patient. One of you also needs to be the witness. You both come to my office on Monday and we'll get the paperwork started."

"Sounds good. We'll say I fell at the club. What else you got?"

Except for a pile of trash the size of Mt. Rushmore and a stench that clung to everything within a 10-mile radius, the vacant lot where Frankie waited for JoJo was picturesque and peaceful in a horror movie kind of way. The only sound, if you didn't count the high pitched squeaking of the hundreds of rats that scurried about the lot, was Frankie's loud cursing as he kicked at the rodents who dared come too close to him and his car. His anger exploded when JoJo pulled up an hour past their meeting time.

"Where the fuck have you been?"

"Do you know how hard it was to find this piece of crap? I had to hunt through every stinking scrap yard in the county for a hunk of junk that isn't traceable, and I don't even know what we're doing here."

"You got a friggin' problem, take it up with the boss. Just do what you were told to do. Get in the car and ram it into the back of my Cadillac."

"Why? Why the fuck am I slamming into your new car with this relic from the Stone Age?"

"Weren't you listening when Vincent told you that he and the doc had a way for all of us to make a shit load of cash."

"I don't like that guy. He's a stronzo."

"Shut the fuck up. You're the stronzo because only an asshole would pass up a sure thing when it comes to making money."

"Yeah. So how we gonna do that?"

Vincent and the doc found a new way to screw the insurance companies and, since we've done well with these scams in the past, there's no reason to doubt them now."

"Okay... just explain how this one works. If I hit you, aren't I responsible for the accident?"

"Vincent's right and I'm wrong. You're not a stronzo. You're a cretino."

"Fuck you."

"Listen. You won't be responsible because we're going to say you were in the car with me. This will be a hit and run. We'll get the Flintstone mobile crushed right after you cream my caddy. No one will ever find it. Now, do you understand?"

# CHAPTER TWELVE

*C*at and Marci arrived at Dr. Michael Vitale's office just as his nurses and receptionist were returning from lunch. Although the waiting room was already full, one quick flash of their badges gained the detectives entry with little more than a few minute's wait.

Vitale's office was impressive in size and expensively decorated. A solid mahogany desk sat upon a nearly room-sized oriental rug. Matching floor to ceiling book cases lined the walls. The shelves held photographs of the good doctor with famous people from the entertainment and political spectrum. The crystal and gold of numerous "good citizen" awards sparkled under inconspicuous recessed spotlights. Michael Vitale rose as Cat and Marci entered and extended a hand in welcome.

"Detectives. Please. Have a seat. How can I help you?"

"We're here about one of your patients. Actually, he's an old friend of yours." Marci sat so she could take notes. Cat continued to stand, smiling at Vitale while she explained their visit. "Vincent Policastro."

"Of course, I know Vincent. We went to high school together."

"And now you'll be going to his funeral."

The expression on Vitale's face melded into a mix of genuine sorrow, shock and fear. It was the fear that most interested Cat and

Marci. When the doctor regained his composure, he advised his receptionist to reschedule his patients and gave his staff the remainder of the day off. Then, he sat, outwardly calm but mentally anxious that the questions he was about to answer would incriminate him in some way.

There had been a day just a few weeks earlier when Michael Vitale thought all his hard work and clever schemes had been for naught. That was the afternoon Vincent, Frankie and JoJo brought the welsher, Johnny Porco, into the office with a plan to get the money he owed... one way or another. Unfortunately, since Vincent and his crew hadn't waited until office hours were over, Michael was fairly certain that the agonizing sounds coming from Porco's throat had been heard in the waiting room. Vitale's staff was savvy enough to know that keeping their heads down and their mouths shut was the best course of action. His patients... Michael had spent many a sleepless night wondering what opinions they had formed.

Johnny Porco was a twerp of a man. He weighed 135 pounds on a stormy day, had a crew cut so severe that anyone running their fingers through his hair would get paper cuts and a pock marked face that resembled the surface of the moon. There was a deep scar on his chin and teeth marks in his left ear where a bar room combatant had bitten away the lobe. He was also badly bruised around his face and upper body. According to Frankie, Johnny's injuries were the result of a freak accident.

**Two hours earlier:**

The diminutive Porco was returning home from the grocery store when he was met by Frankie and JoJo standing on the sidewalk in front of his rundown apartment building.

"Hey, Johnny. Just the man we were looking for. Let me give you a hand with those bags." Frankie's act of kindness had all the subtlety of a snake coiling around its victim's throat.

"Frankie. JoJo. Hey... no help needed. I got this." Johnny Porco fumbled in his pocket for his apartment key as he edged his way backward to the front stoop.

"Come on. Give me one of the bags. No need for you to carry all those groceries by yourself." Frankie's grip on the paper sack did not allow for any resistance. "Let us see what you got in here?"

"Oh, man... how could you?" JoJo peaked into the grocery bag and, feigning shock, cast a look in Porco's direction that immediately filled his weasel eyes with shame. "Ragu? What the hell were you thinking? An Italian using jarred spaghetti sauce is an infamia!" JoJo hefted the jar in his hand.

"I ain't got time to cook. Been busy."

"You got time to give us the money you owe Vincent, you piece of shit?" Frankie asked with a smile.

Like a jackrabbit, Porco loped to the front door. Frankie dropped the bag of groceries on the sidewalk. He and JoJo set off in pursuit. Taking two steps at a time, Porco managed to insert his key into the lock. Quickly slipping through the opening, he used his shoulder to push the door closed. Porco was quick but JoJo was quicker. He stuck his foot into the space between the door and the jamb preventing it from closing. He still had the jar of Ragu in his hand.

"Don't make matters worse. Just open the fucking door," JoJo yelled.

Porco turned and ran up the stairs leading to his second-floor apartment. JoJo and Frankie followed him at a more casual pace. They laughed as Porco slipped on the top step and momentarily lost his balance.

Just as Porco reached his apartment door. JoJo took careful aim and threw the jar of Ragu, hitting him in the back of the head and knocking him to the ground. "Damn. I'm good, aren't I, Johnny boy?" he smirked.

JoJo and Frankie took their time reaching Porco's prone body.

"You never answered my question," Frankie said, kicking Johnny in the ribs. "Where's the fucking money you owe Vincent?"

"I got nothing. I'm sorry."

"Not sorry enough," Frankie reached under Porco's arms and lifted him off the ground. He kneed him in the stomach and Porco again fell to the ground.

"You see what happens when you make Frankie angry? Why'd you make him do that?" JoJo pulled the moaning man to his feet and put his arm around his shoulders.

"Come on. Lean on me. I don't want you to slip on any of that delicious spaghetti sauce that's all over the floor."

"Please don't kill me." Porco cried, his face covered in a mix of blood and tears.

"I'm not going to kill you. Not yet, at least. We still need you to pay back the money you owe." JoJo led Johnny back toward the staircase. "Let's go see what Vincent wants to do with you."

Just as they reached the top step, JoJo shoved Johnny head first down the stairs.

"Ah, shit, man," JoJo yelled after Porco's tumbling form. "I told you to be careful. Spaghetti sauce can be slippery."

Frankie stood beside JoJo and watched as Porco came to rest in the hallway below. "Freak accident."

"Yeah. Freaky," JoJo chuckled as he walked down the stairs. Standing above Porco's prone form, he kicked him in the ribs. "Come on. Get up!"

"My head... Jesus, I think you cracked my skull."

"You got a headache?" Frankie feigned concerned. "I know just the doctor to help you."

Both Michael Vitale and Vincent were smiling as they listened to Frankie's and JoJo's version of events. Johnny Porco was silent... pain keeping him mute except for the groans that escaped his lips every few seconds.

Vitale studied Johnny's face assessing his injuries. "It's just a shame he didn't break his nose. It would make for a much stronger case. The more injuries; the more money."

With no further encouragement needed, Frankie stepped in front of Johnny and punched him dead center with all his might. It was the resulting scream that Michael Vitale feared his patients sitting in the waiting room had heard.

"Dr. Vitale, we've been told that you and Vincent Policastro were business partners. Is that true?" Cat Leigh stood tall, staring down at Michael Vitale, who was seated uncomfortably behind his desk.

"Reciprocity is the foundation of most successful businesses. Detective Leigh. It is true that if I have a patient who is moving into or out of the state, I will recommend Crotone Moving. In turn, should someone Vincent knows require medical assistance, he will suggest they come to see me. If that's what you call business partners, then I guess the answer is "Yes.""

"In reviewing our files, your name came up often on suspicious automobile accident reports… those that appeared to be staged crashes."

"Was I the driver of any of those cars? Was I present at the scene of the accidents?"

"Not as far as we know."

"Then what association, other than being a much sought after orthopedist, would I have with any of those cases?"

"You make a lot of money from those crashes. And your lawyer, Marvin Manker… he makes a lot of money as well. His name appears as often as does yours in our case files."

"It is against the law for a doctor to recommend a lawyer to a patient so I never show favoritism. In fact, whenever a patient asks for advice, I hand them the business cards of all of the attorneys… well, all those who are good at their job. There are approximately four who are excellent personal injury lawyers. I'm sure their names come up in your files quite often as well."

"Not as often as Mr. Manker."

"Then that is a testament to the intelligence of my patients. They do their research. Anyone looking Marvin up on the internet will find that he is highly recommended with a success record exceeded by no other attorney in south Florida."

"Obviously, you and Attorney Manker have a good thing going."

"Were police reports filed on these accidents, Detective?"

"Yes."

"Well, it isn't my job to authenticate those reports. That's your job. I have to take my patient's word that they were in an accident and that they are injured."

CHAPTER THIRTEEN

*A*fter their extended interview with Michael Vitale, Cat and Marci were forced to speed across town so as not to be late for their meeting with Detectives Moe DiLorenzo and Damian Mack. The purpose of the meeting was to consult with G regarding the autopsies he had performed on Gamalial Cohn and Vincent Policastro.

Entering the morgue, they were brought up short by the overpowering smell of disinfectant. Decaying bodies they could handle, but the heavy scent of ammonia always brought tears to their eyes. Moe and Mack were waiting for them in the reception area. Moe had a handkerchief pressed to his face.

"Why can't they make lemon scented cleansers?" Moe said to no one in particular, his voice muffled by the cotton cloth pressed to his nose and mouth.

"They do… just not for morgues. If you want essential oils, visit a boutique, not a body shop." Damian Mack enjoyed tormenting his partner over his sensitivity to smells.

"Body shop? Aren't you the clever one."

"And you're such a whiner. Last week it was the tire department at Costco that had you sneezing. Why don't you just wear a clothespin on your nose?"

"Go fu…"

"Hey, guys. Sorry we're late." Cat cut the verbal exchange between the two partners short. "Is G here yet?"

Dr. Mark "G" Geschwer's many years as Medical Examiner had given him a deep insight into the fears and foibles of the human race… both the living and the dead… and he used that knowledge to assuage the jitters felt by all those who entered his domain. Whether the person coming to meet him was a family member of the recently deceased or a law enforcement officer seeking answers to an open case, G went out of his way to make the visit as painless as possible. Except for the smell.

Expecting a dark and dingy environment—the depressingly dull greens and browns that usually dominated these underground lairs—visitors were often surprised to find themselves in a world where soft yellow walls played host to images of the great comedians past and present. G was partial to the old timers—Red Skelton, Henny Young-man, Jerry Lewis, Jack Benny and Bob Hope—but he also had great respect for the newer, more adventurous comedians who had thumbed their noses at propriety and opened the door for comedy based on life as people actually lived it.

George Carlin, Richard Pryor, Robin Williams, Steve Martin, Eddie Murphy and Chris Rock were some of his favorites. Their faces smiled back at visitors from publicity shots and movie posters which covered every inch of wall space. No matter how heavy the burden one felt when entering the morgue, the weight on their shoulders felt decidedly lighter when they left.

For first timers, the sterile, silent world where the dead revealed their secrets by exposing themselves in a deeply invasive way could be disconcerting. In an attempt to breathe a little life into the stillness that hung heavy in the air, G often dressed in outlandish outfits that were more clown costume than business suit. His starched white medical jacket seemed a stark contrast to the rainbow of colors that were a part of his daily wardrobe.

While known for treating the bodies on his autopsy table with abso-lute respect, G was also acknowledged for using humor the way most doctors used band aids. His less than perfect impersonations of Jack Benny and Rodney Dangerfield were hilarious, but it was his attempts to mimic Jerry Lewis that usually had department personnel rolling their eyes. When asked why he allowed himself to look the fool, he said with total sincerity, "People don't hurt when they are laughing."

Cat, Marci and their colleagues had long since stopped being surprised by the contradictions they found at G's home away from home. They took comfort in the pastel color of the exterior halls while being deeply aware of the delicate work being done inside the stainless steel and glass rooms where the dead uttered their last words.

G appeared at the doors to his inner sanctum and motioned for the four detectives to follow him. Rather than turning left into the autopsy suites, he led them down a long corridor to the loading dock. Standing just inside the doors was Captain Constantine. Her unexpected appearance brought the four horsemen of the PBSO up short.

"Captain?" Marci's voice held an edge of uncertainty.

"Apologies, detectives. While I know your meeting with the good doctor is important, we have things to discuss. Please follow me."

"Where are we going?" While Moe, Mack and Marci moved in behind their captain, Cat stayed planted where she was standing.

"I can't tell you that but I promise that if you come with me, you will be... maybe not pleasantly surprised... but definitely surprised in some manner. Dr. Geschwer, please join us."

The five PBSO officers and G moved en masse out the doors and took their assigned seats in the black SUV parked at the curb. The vehicle's windows were tinted so dark that only an owl could see in or out. No one spoke as the car moved quickly through the streets of downtown West Palm Beach. Eventually, the silent driver pulled into a garage in an isolated part of town and the rolling metal door slammed closed before the car engine had even been killed.

While the unexpected *kidnapping* by Captain Constantine had Moe, Mack, Cat and Marci off balance, it was the four people waiting inside the garage that really shocked them. Two of those people were wearing the standard issue off-the-rack dark suits favored by Federal agents. They stood like soldiers on either side of two other people – one male and one female - who were more casually dressed. When Cat's and Marci's eyes adjusted to the dim lighting and they saw who the other two people were their mouths dropped open. In fact, upon seeing and recognizing the man and the woman standing before them, Cat and Marci were struck speechless.

"Detectives," Captain Constantine stepped forward to make the introductions. "I know you've already met Agent Annette Anderson aka Jeannetta Jordan. And this is Agent Clark Costanza aka Joey Jericho aka JoJo."

It took Cat and Marci a few seconds to wrap their heads around the fact that two of the people they suspected of being involved in the murder of Vincent Policastro were actually undercover agents with the FBI. Agent Anderson was the first to offer an explanation for their involvement.

"My apologies, Detectives, for not being more forthcoming when we met at The Firehouse. My goal in telling you about the Feds sudden appearance at the club and the placement of listening devices was a warning that our conversation was being recorded... not by the Bureau... by Ernie. Clark and I have been working together for a few years now. We've been gathering information for a RICO case against the Policastro empire. The last thing we expected was for Vincent to be murdered."

Clark Costanza stepped in with more on their involvement. "The surprise visits by the Bureau were planned to keep Ernie and Vincent off balance. We didn't really need listening devices because Annette and I were trusted and knew most of what was going on."

"Ernie considers the Feds 'predictable,' so we've tried to live up to our reputation where he's concerned." Annette Anderson smiled broadly.

"After each raid, I removed the ears planted by our agents," Clark continued. "However, I was careful not to touch the devices that Ernie had stashed around the club. There is one under every table in the dining room… even the table where you sat to interrogate Annette. Ernie and Vincent have made a fortune blackmailing people with bits of information picked up by eavesdropping on private conversations."

"I've known Clark for years…," Captain Constantine joined the conversation, "… so when Gamalial Cohen was murdered, he was the first person I turned to for help. I knew the Feds had to be watching the Policastro empire carefully. I never suspected they had an agent on the inside. When I called Clark, I was merely hoping he could fish around and find out what, if anything, the Bureau knew that could help with our case. Imagine my surprise when I saw his photo in the case file. I didn't know about Annette until today. Anyway, now we're working together."

"Since we wanted to know the outcome of the autopsies on Cohen, his family and Vincent Policastro, meeting here and including the doc seemed a good idea. Plus, this is much safer than the morgue… we know there are no recording devices in use." Clark Costanza waved his arm as assurance that the entire building had been swept and secured.

Moe and Mack stepped forward, hands outstretched. "It's nice to meet you, Agents."

Moe took a chance that Agent Anderson would have a sense of humor and commented on the tight short skirt and tight low- cut tee shirt she was wearing. "Have to say, Agent Anderson, you are a beautiful addition to the staff at The Firehouse."

Annette Anderson put her thumb to her mouth, licked it, and placed it on her hip while making a sizzling sound. Everyone laughed.

Cat and Marci were still glued to the floor, unsure whether they were pissed off or pleased that the Feds were involved in their investigation.

"If you are all ready, we've set up a small office where we can review Dr. Geschwer's autopsy results. This way, please."

One of the unnamed agents led the way deeper into the garage.

The small office where the law enforcement officers sat to hear the results of G's autopsies had none of the warmth of his actual office at the morgue. There, the first thing a visitor saw upon sitting down was the inscribed plaque hanging on the wall behind his desk.

*"No matter what your heartache may be,*
*laughing helps you forget it for a few seconds."*

The quote was attributed to Red Skelton, and the sentiment behind the words was one that G took seriously and practiced daily. However, while he knew that laughter had its place in a murder investigation, he also knew that this was not the time for even a small chuckle.

As he was about to sit down, G noticed the poster on the office wall -- a holdover from the garage's days as a chop shop. On it, a naked woman was spread eagled over the fender of a red 1953 Buick convertible. She was smiling, her head turned to the camera as she licked her lips. The inscription on the poster read:

*Full Service Garage – Our men have the biggest tools and our women know how to use them!*

G pulled it down and threw it in the corner before he took his seat. He looked at Cat and Marci apologetically. The detectives nodded their acknowledgment of his desire to always be respectful of both the living and dead. It was one of the things they loved most about him.

"Let's start with Attorney Cohen, his wife and son. All three were killed with the same gun—a .357 Magnum. These were close contact kills even though a .357 doesn't need to be pressed against the skull to inflict a fatal injury. Cohen was shot in the back of the head while sitting at his desk. His body was moved to the lake on the golf course but why is out of my purview. Perhaps, his killer thought attorney Cohen would make a delicious dinner for Andy the alligator. Since there wasn't so much as a tooth mark on Cohen's body, I'm assuming Andy extended professional courtesy.

Mrs. Cohen and her son were shot in their beds. There were no signs of a struggle. I believe they were both sound asleep and never heard their killer approach.

The severing of the tongues is especially interesting. Both were done post mortem. They were clean cuts... quick and precise. The blade was surgically sharp, perhaps one owned by Cohen and used on his hunting expeditions. No such weapon was found at either scene. The switching of the tongues was, I believe, a message... one I can only speculate upon."

Clark Costanza raised a finger in polite interruption. "I can explain the reason for the tongue switch. You're correct. It was a message but to whom, we're not sure. To give you a more complete picture of what we think happened, I need to go back to October.

As you are aware, Maria Policastro holds a high stakes poker game the third Sunday of every month at the Ritz Carlton in Manalapan. Those games go on into the wee hours of the morning. Since Vincent doesn't play cards, which is not to say he doesn't gamble, he uses those opportunities to fly to New York and check on his business interests. On October 17th, he arrived back in Florida around midnight and stopped at Crotone Moving where he was supposed to meet with Ernie. Only Frankie and I were waiting. Here's where some of the answers we are all seeking lay.

Frankie told Vincent that Ernie was chasing down a scum bag named Johnny Porco. Porco owed Vincent a lot of money. In reality, Ernie was spying on Vincent's wife. For some time, he had suspected that there was more than friendship between Maria and Dr. Vitale. He had even enlisted Gamalial Cohen's help to find out what was going on.

Cohen's wife and Maria Policastro were good friends... very good friends. Mrs. Cohen was also her husband's best friend... or, at least, he thought so, and that, I believe, was why he died. The severed tongues suggest that Cohen broke the cardinal rule not to involve family, especially wives, in business matters. My guess is he either told his wife about Ernie's suspicions and/or asked his wife to watch Maria for signs of an affair. Mrs. Cohen most likely told Maria. Whoever killed the Cohen family also killed Vincent. Maybe it was Maria.

Maybe it was Vitale. But I'm pretty sure from the nervous way Ernie is acting, he thinks he's next on the list."

"And the Cohen's son? He was just... what... thirteen?" Cat's anger that one so young had died due to the stupidity of their parents was obvious.

"Collateral damage." Annette Anderson was equally angry at the callousness of the crime. "He might have overheard something and the killer wasn't taking any chances."

"Or...," Clark Costanza interjected, "it could just have been old school mafia mentality. Leave no one behind to seek revenge."

Marci had listened intently to all the federal agents had said. "Is it possible we could use Ernie's nerves to our advantage. He doesn't know that the two of you are undercover. That's to our advantage. What if a federal prosecutor told him that the Bureau has uncovered enough proof to put him in jail for a long time.

The prosecutor could tell him that if he works with us to catch Vincent's killer, the government will go easy on him on the racketeering charges?"

"We want Ernie just as badly as you want Vincent's killer. I'm not sure our Chief will agree to let him off the hook."

"Who said you were actually going to let him off the hook. These guys are scam artists. Can't we take a page out of their book and figure out a way to get two... or three... birds with one stone?"

# CHAPTER FOURTEEN

$\mathcal{T}$he first step to putting the joint Bureau/PBSO plan into action was a search warrant for Gamalial Cohen's home office. The attorney's files had initially been searched immediately upon finding the family murdered, but now that the focus of the investigation had narrowed some, another look was required. The search warrant was just a precaution... an attempt to make sure that all the I's were dotted and T's crossed should the investigation result in an indictment. If Cohen had uncovered information linking Maria Policastro to Michael Vitale, it could be the proof needed to bring them to trial and conviction.

Since Mack and Moe were assigned to Cohen's murder case, they prepared the paperwork and submitted their affidavits to a judge. The warrant was approved in less than eight hours. Signed document in hand, Moe, Mack, Cat and Marci along with Officer Keith McKinney arrived at the Cohen home at 6:30 the following morning. No Federal agents were present... an attempt to keep the connection between the two law enforcement agencies as hush hush as possible. Since the house had been sealed as part of a crime scene, no one was there to impede their efforts.

Recognizing that their entire case could hinge on what might be found in Gamalial Cohen's file cabinets and desk drawers, the officers used great care when removing and reading through the paperwork. This was not a search and destroy mission but, rather, one where cautious deliberation would be taken to preserve every document no matter how insignificant or irrelevant. Mack and Moe started with the long line of five drawer high storage units that filled the walk in closet in Cohen's office suite. Officer McKinney took charge of the floor to ceiling bookcases, an unenviable task. Cat tackled Cohen's desk while Marci headed for the wall-length credenza that served as a display space for family photographs and cherished gifts from his son. The hardened lump of clay studded with seashells and imprinted with the younger Cohen's handprint held prominence in the center of the credenza's polished black walnut top.

Hours of painstaking and sometimes boring review followed. Each and every scrap residing inside the carefully labeled manila folders which were further nestled inside green universal hanging folders was read and reread. Cohen was nothing if not organized. If he had, indeed, found evidence of unfaithfulness or chicanery between Maria Poli-castro and Michael Vitale, he had stashed it well. It was nearing noon when Marci's voice rang out, encouraging Moe, Mack, McKinney and Cat to join her on the floor where she was sitting cross legged surrounded by papers. The credenza had been pulled away from the wall on one end just enough for Marci's arm to reach behind and retrieve what had been hidden there.

Among the documents found were copies of financial statements listing the numerous deposits made by Maria with a private tax and asset securitization group based in New York City. The group had ties to offshore banking. The amount of money Maria had earned playing cards was mind boggling—well into the high eight figure mark. Even more surprising was Michael Vitale's name as co-account holder. An envelope containing photographs of Maria and Vitale in compromising positions was the most condemning and the least appealing, especially to Marci who hated invading someone's intimate moments even if those moments were proof that a crime had been committed.

The most eye opening document—one that clearly pointed a finger at Maria and Michael Vitale as co-conspirators in Vincent Policastro's murder and the death of Gamalial Cohen— was a signed affidavit stating that Vitale was the father of Maria's and Vincent's 15-year-old daughter, Teresa. There was also a copy of a birth certificate listing Vincent as the father. Quickly doing the math in her head, Cat laid out a timeframe.

"So, since Maria was 18 when she and Vincent married, and she's about 40 now, that would mean that the daughter was born approximately seven years into her marriage to Vincent. Considering that the dates on these financial statements are current and Vitale's name has never been removed, one would have to assume that the affair has been going on a long time."

"Take a look at this." Moe held up a sheaf of papers which appeared to be a transcript of notes taken by Cohen. "According to statements Cohen got from numerous folks in the old neighborhood... that means New Jersey not Sicily... Maria and Vitale have had a hot and heavy relationship since they were teenagers. Vitale's sister, Margie Maggiano, who obviously doesn't like Maria, told Cohen '... that bitch and my brother were screwing in the coat room at my wedding. I don't think Vincent knew but, if he didn't, he was the only one in the dark. Once a whore—always a whore.'

"Is it possible a man as savvy as Vincent Policastro could have been cuckolded by his wife and best friend all these years and never suspected?" Marci was justifiably doubtful.

"More than possible...," Moe continued looking through the transcripts as he spoke. "Vitale must have recorded his conversations with Vincent. Remember, Maria said Vincent hurt his back and was going to Vitale for treatment. Well, listen to this exchange."

Vitale: What did you do to yourself?

Vincent: I fell outta bed.

Vitale: Fell out of bed, huh. Still the same old Vincent, I see.

Vincent: Maria is hard to resist even after all these years.

Vitale: She does have a way of taking hold of your heart and never letting go.

Vincent: That she does.

Vitale: How's the family?

Vincent: I can't believe my little girl isn't a little girl anymore. I keep thinking of what Maria and I were like at that age and I want to lock her in a closet until she's 50.

Vitale: I know exactly how you feel. My son just turned 20 and my daughter is 15.

Vincent: Yeah. Our little girls were born around the same time. You got a rich man's family.

Vitale: So they say.

"There's more but you get the idea," Moe said as he put the transcripts into a manila folder for safe keeping. "Interesting... yes? Vitale was also married while screwing Maria. His wife was pregnant at the same time Maria was pregnant. Must have been one hell of a soap opera."

"Vincent Policastro ran a multi-million dollar far-flung criminal empire." Marci sounded incredulous by what she had just heard. "People cowered when he walked into the room. How could one woman hold so much control over him?"

"There is nothing more deceptive than an obvious fact." Cat smiled slyly at Marci.

"Thank you, Sherlock Holmes. And what is that fact?"

"Vincent loved Maria. He truly, truly loved her."

# CHAPTER FIFTEEN

*W*ith information provided by Agents Costanza and Anderson, the officers from the Strategic Operations Division of the Palm Beach County Sheriff's Office, which included special operations and violent crimes, raided Ernie Mastrianno's house. When they arrived, they found Ernie and Frankie sitting in the kitchen eating dinner. In the living room, three unidentified men sat at a long folding table surrounded by canvas bags filled with quarters. The men dumped the coins into counting machines and rolled them into $10.00 paper wrappers. Along one wall, plastic milk cartons filled with the coin rolls were stacked three high. Along another wall what appeared to be dollar bills were stacked high and wide. From a distance the bills appeared to be legitimate, but a closer examination revealed that George Washington's face had been replaced with a pornographic image of three people having sex.

For the sake of credibility, JoJo (aka Agent Costanza) had been nabbed an hour earlier while he was feeding phony dollar bills into a change machine at a local laundromat. PBSO detectives had followed him as he made his rounds, videotaping him filling the canvas bags with the ill-gotten gains. When the time was right, they arrested him and brought him to the main detention center on Gun Club Road in West Palm Beach.

A thorough search of Ernie's small guest room/office uncovered a wall safe hidden behind a framed poster of Al Pacino in the Godfather Part II movie. Actually, there were four framed posters on the wall—all of them heralding the popular trilogy which chronicled the rise of a poor Sicilian immigrant to the head of a large and powerful Mafia family. The safe was easily opened once *pressure* was exerted on Ernie to reveal the combination. Inside were two velvet bags, one containing large, beautifully cut diamonds and the other holding rings, bracelets and necklaces devoid of stones. Signed and notarized appraisals and riders to Ernie's homeowners insurance policy covering the each of the jewelry items were also found in the safe. A quick scan of the paperwork revealed that the bling had been bought, insured and lost in relatively quick succession.

"How much do you want to bet that the diamond bracelet Ernie gave his mom to sit here in the house and fool the Feds is one of these gem-less wonders?" Cat dangled two tennis bracelets from the tip of her finger.

While Cat and Marci remained in charge of the raid at the Mastrianno residence, Moe and Mack handled the same duties at the coordinated raid on The Firehouse. Among the stolen items recovered from the kitchen's walk-in freezer were five 20-pound slabs of filet mignon, 12 pounds of Alaskan king crab legs and crates of lobster tails and Russian caviar—all part of the inventory from high-jacked food trucks along Interstate I-95.

The Firehouse was immediately closed to the public. Any patrons who had not run for the exits when the police entered were allowed to leave once they had shown some form of identification and provided contact information for future questioning. Jeannetta Jordan (aka Agent Annette Anderson) was rounded up with the rest of the staff and carted off to jail.

Ernie Mastrianno, the now head of the Policastro crime family, was handcuffed and brought to the West Palm Beach branch office of the U.S. Attorney for the Southern District of Florida. Despite the late hour, Frederick Willard, the chief federal law enforcement officer for the area, was waiting with a "We've got you now smile." His gray/green eyes fairly sparkled as he offered Ernie a seat before his desk.

Willard was a career politician. He began his service as U.S. Attorney for the Southern District of Florida after being nominated by President Barack Obama and confirmed by the Senate earlier in the year. As U.S. Attorney, he was the chief federal law enforcement officer for the District—a stepping stone to greater glory.

Attorney Willard had graduated law school at the top of his class in 1990. Always ambitious, he began his career clerking for a highly regarded judge in the 11th Circuit—a prestigious position given only to the best and the brightest graduate from Yale Law School. Afterward, he joined a prestigious Dade County law firm but quickly realized that his true love was public service. His new found purpose took him to the Department of Justice and, eventually, he came full circle, returning to Miami as Assistant U.S. Attorney. In that capacity, he was responsible for some extremely high profile crimes, including international money laundering, health care fraud, narcotics, international human rights abuses, immigration, and firearms offenses. Tonight, mouth watering with the anticipated sweet taste of success, he set his sights on Tallahassee and the Governor's mansion.

Back at the PBSO Main Detention Center on Gun Club Road, Agent Anderson was photographed and fingerprinted along with the dancers, wait staff and kitchen help that had been rounded up at The Firehouse. One by One, they were interrogated by a PBSO detective; Anderson giving her statements in the comfort of the Captain Constantine's office.

Clark Costanza, who had been deftly moved from a holding cell to the office, was also present as was Special Agent in Charge Trevor Hoerler from the FBI Miami Field Office. Detectives Moe Di Lorenzo and Damian Mack joined them. They all waited anxiously to hear from Cat and Marci as to whether Ernie Mastrianno had accepted the terms of the plea deal being offered him by United States Attorney Frederick Willard.

Recognizing that Mastrianno was the key to arresting and convicting Maria Policastro and Michael Vitale in the murder of Vincent Policastro, Attorney Willard chose his words carefully. He knew that Ernie's testimony would play a decisive role in putting Maria and Michael away for life. Letting Ernie go completely unpunished for his crimes was out of the question. Instead, Willard offered him a sentence of five years in a minimum security prison near his home so that Momma Mastrianno could visit often. There was also the promise that he would not be called to testify and his identity would be redacted in transcripts of the case. Ernie accepted.

Of course, all these promises were dependent upon Maria and Michael appearing before a judge and admitting their involvement. They would then need to accept whatever deal was offered them by Attorney Willard—most likely life in a general population cell block instead of death row. If the evidence provided by Ernie was damning enough, there was little chance the love birds would turn down the deal.

Before presenting his offer to Mastrianno, Attorney Willard met with federal agents and urged them to agree to the somewhat lenient sentence. Five years, he assured them, was not a long time to put their investigation on hold. Additionally, since Frankie Fortunato and Joey Jericho (Agent Costanza) would run the business in Ernie's absence—following orders delivered from behind prison bars—the Bureau would continue to build a strong case and, eventually, take down one of the nation's best-known crime families. Everyone agreed.

Once Ernie Mastrianno had placed his John Hancock on the plea deal and shared his wealth of information with investigators, a search warrant was gotten for Michael Vitale's office. Again, the Feds kept a low profile, allowing detectives from the Palm Beach County Sheriff's Office to handle the search and seizure.

At a midnight strategic planning session that lasted past sunrise, Cat, Marci, Moe, Mack, the feds and Attorney Willard laid out different scenarios for proving "… who killed Vincent and how." Since Maria had not tested positive for gun powder residue on the day of Vincent's death, she was immediately ruled out as the person who actually pulled the trigger. The question then became "If Michael Vitale killed Vincent, how did he get into the bedroom?"

A review of surveillance tapes from the hotel showed the exterior hallways devoid of human presence in the hours between Vincent's return to the suite and the cleaning crew arriving. There were no suspicious fingerprints on door handles or surfaces inside or outside the room. None of the trace evidence that had been collected pointed to Michael Vitale being present. The murder scene was clean except for the expected debris left by the card players.

Cat, Marci and assorted colleagues arrived at Michael Vitale's office before patient hours began. His nursing staff was already on site and along with the receptionist, they were taken to PBSO headquarters for questioning. An officer was stationed at the door to keep the ailing and injured from entering and guarantee that the good doctor did not do an about face when he stepped off the elevator.

Much as they had done at the Cohen home, the officers divided the task of searching the office. This time the evidence they were looking for presented itself in short order. Cat pulled on the deep file drawer in Vitale's desk and felt it catch on something that made forward movement difficult. She yanked and tugged at the drawer but only managed to open it a few millimeters. With the help of her colleagues, she cleared the writing surface of its assortment of business and personal items and upended the desk. Taped to the bottom of the drawer was Marco Molina's leather bound notebook.

A quick glance at the contents of Molina's diary of deceits was enough to send two officers to the Ritz Carlton to pick him up for questioning. Upon inquiring as to his whereabouts, they were told that the diminutive concierge had been missing in action for a week. He had given no notice of his decision to leave his job. His landlord had not been advised of his intent to vacant his apartment and a search of his residence presented the picture of a man, perhaps, away on vacation but definitely not gone for good.

CHAPTER SIXTEEN

*M*arco Molina was nowhere to be found. His friends in the United States had not heard from him. His family in Italy were unaware that anything was wrong. His disappearance was much like a vanishing act... here one minute and gone the next. Even a puff of smoke left a bigger trail than did Molina's departure.

The one thing that was confirmed by a search of his apartment was that he had gotten in over his head with the Policastro family. He got greedy and greed is never a character trait that puts a person in a position of power when dealing with the predators of this world.

Hidden under a loose floorboard under Molina's bed were security tapes from the Ritz Carlton taken the night Vincent Policastro was murdered. They clearly showed Molina letting Dr. Michael Vitale into the bedroom portion of the suite where Maria Policastro had held her poker game. Based on notations in Molina's journal, he had demanded far too much money from Vitale for the part he played in the crime. Vitale no doubt balked and, realizing that Molina now was a loose end that needed to be eliminated, had killed him.

Despite an in depth investigation, Cat and Marci were never able to discover what had happened to the swishy little man who had hoped to return to Italy as a wealthy retiree. It was possible he had gone home and was in seclusion. However, a better supposition was that any return to Positano was done in an urn and that his ashes were now floating on the Tyrrhenian Seas. Either way, he had gotten his wish.

"Little did Molina know that he would prove Thomas Wolfe wrong," Marci commented to Cat when they closed the missing person portion of the Policastro case. "One way or the other, you can go home again."

Based on the surveillance tapes, Michael Vitale was arrested and charged with the murder of Vincent Policastro. Cat, Marci and three uniformed officers descended upon his office like a low flying cloud of bats dressed in black Kevlar vests. They took no heed of the patients waiting in the outer office or of the receptionist who stuck her head through the sliding glass partition and ordered, "You can't go in there." A snarling "Sit down!" from Marci was enough to make her obediently pull her head back in and slide the partition closed.

Michael Vitale looked genuinely surprised when his office door opened and Cat and Marci entered followed by the police officers. Cat held the arrest warrant high in her hand, while Marci, dangling hand cuffs, strode to Vitale's side and yanked him out of his chair. "Dr. Michael Vitale, you are under arrest for the murder of Vincent Policastro. You have the right to remain silent. Anything you say can and will be used against you in a court of law. You have the right to an attorney. If you cannot afford an attorney, one will be provided for you. Do you understand the rights I have just read to you? With these rights in mind, do you wish to speak to me?"

Vitale remained momentarily mute. Then, he demanded, "I want my attorney called immediately."

"We'll do that the minute we get you back to the precinct." Cat stood beside the eyes wide and, obviously, delighted patient. She touched him on the arm to get his attention. "You can leave now. I'd suggest you find another physician for whatever ails you. Dr. Vitale won't be treating anyone for a very long time."

Michael Vitale was also charged with the murders of Gamalial

Cohen and his family. Thanks to Marco Molina's numerous notes, it was revealed that Vitale was aware of Cohen's interest in his relationship with Maria, and he was furious. Fear of retribution spurred him to kill Cohen before Cohen could reveal what he knew to Vincent. With an inflated sense of altruism, he also believed he was protecting Maria from Vincent's jealous reaction should he learn that his wife had been unfaithful.

"When I was a little girl," Cat told Marci, "my grandfather would often say, 'You can take the boy out of the old neighborhood, but you can't take the criminal out of the old boy.' I guess he was right. Vitale broke one of the Mafia's ten commandments, 'Never look at the wives of friends.'"

Because Cohen had ignored the dictate not to talk to wives and children about "family" business, he had put himself, his wife and his son in danger. Mrs. Cohen, who was somewhat innocent and naïve when it came to matters of the heart, had asked her best friend, Maria Policastro, if she was having an affair. She did this because she did not believe for a minute that Maria would be unfaithful to Vincent—the man she claimed to love with all her heart. Maria, of course, repeated that conversation to Vitale who moved quickly to silence the Cohens. Why Ernie Mastrianno was still alive was a mystery, especially since it was Ernie who had asked Cohen to look into the illicit relationship.

Hard as they tried, Cat and Marci were unable to directly tie Maria to the killing. Their gut told them that the decision to kill Vincent had been jointly made by both Maria and Vitale, probably so that they could take over control of the Policastro empire. No doubt their plan had been for Vincent to be the face of the organization. Maria would be the brains. However, with Vitale most likely spending a good portion of his remaining years on death row, Maria would wear that crown alone. There was no question that Ernie Mastrianno would challenge her authority. As Vincent Policastro's right-hand man, the position of godfather belonged to him. Maria's reputation for shrewdness being well known, there was no doubt that she would fight tooth and nail to hold onto her position of power. The war had just begun.

Marci and Cat knew that the FBI would be watching Ernie Mastri-anno closely. The identities of undercover Agents Annette Anderson and Clark Costanza were still secure. Only time would tell whether another joint task force between the FBI and the PBSO was in the cards.

# CHAPTER SEVENTEEN

*W*ith Michael Vitale behind bars and many months to go before the District Attorney would be ready to try the case against him for the murders of Vincent Policastro and Gamalial Cohen, Cat and Marci looked forward to a few *sleep in* mornings and afternoons spent with their families. They were still heavily involved in investigating the death of Governor Gardner but had been temporarily sidelined while awaiting toxicology results from the medical examiner's office. When they went to bed at 10 pm on the Thursday night prior to Vitale's arraignment, they put their cell phones on vibrate so as not to disturb their husbands should a call come in. And, of course, it did just one hour later.

Stumbling their way to their respective bathrooms, they answered the call in the dark and whispered their questions and responses to the dispatcher. After a quick shower, Cat exited her front door and walked to where Marci was already waiting in the driveway. Since confronting and killing Robert Bridgeman on the porch of her home five years ago, Cat and Kevin had taken the precaution of surrounding their property with a fence and a gate that required a code to enter. Two attempts on Cat's life in one year were enough and, since one attempt was made in her front yard, they realized it was time to accept that the dangers of the job did not end when off duty. Marci knew the gate code by heart and, being aware that Cat relived the moment when Bridgeman stepped out of the shadows with a machete in his hand, she made it a point to always be waiting whenever they got a call in the hours before the sun broke across the horizon.

As the partners drove through the still busy streets on their way to the Palm Beach County Convention Center on Okeechobee Boulevard, they discussed what they knew so far. Both Palm Beach County Sheriff Mike Brickshaw and Captain

Constantine were guests at the annual United States Conference of Mayors at which West Palm Beach Mayor Jerrold Morolo was co-chair of the Mayors Water Council. The mayors of Sarasota and Orlando also held prominent positions at the three-day event, respectively serving as co-chairs of the Veteran's Affairs Task Force and the Educational Excellence Task Force. Scheduled as keynote speakers were the mayors of New York City, Boston and Dallas. What little-verified information they had came via a game of telephone – the Captain to the dispatcher to the detectives on call. To the best of their knowledge, no one was dead but pandemonium reigned in the ballroom. Someone as yet unknown to them had infiltrated the event posing as a waiter and was captured when he tried to poison the drinking water with what was assumed to be polonium.

Cat and Marci had attended enough locally held conventions to know that these events always included the requisite gourmet dinner supplied by one of the five star restaurants on Palm Beach Island, a top tier comedian to lighten the mood and a few very high profile dignitaries whose speeches were intended to bring the gathering back to its actual purpose – raising money for their political causes and pushing party agendas while pretending to be concerned about the country, the needs of each state and the people residing in those states.

Mayor Morolo had been honored with a seat on the dais along with the current Governor of Florida Scott Rickman and the two senators who represented Florida in Washington, D.C. In the audience were the chairs of the Democratic and Republican National Committees and most of the 27 representatives from Florida's 435 congressional districts.

When Governor Gardner died as a result of ingesting polonium-210, Cat and Marci became experts in what was often referred to as "the perfect poison." Polonium, they learned, was not just an immensely powerful poison, it was also almost impossible to detect in the body unless doctors knew to specifically look for it. The reason for this was very simple. The outward symptoms of polonium poisoning mimicked thallium ingestion, an element found in rat poison. Hair loss, severe nausea, vomiting and diarrhea as well as blinding headaches took doctors on a familiar diagnostic path rather than suggesting a more exotic route. This ability to conceal its presence among simpler, more commonly found poisons, made polonium a secret weapon without a match.

If not for G's attention to detail, Governor Gardner's death would have been reported as poisoning by rodent repellent, perhaps, as a result of the restaurant having had its monthly pest control service. Initially, G was grudgingly satisfied that the Governor's death had been accidental. However, nagging doubt forced him to go over the results of his autopsy time and time again. A firm believer in gut instinct, he ordered a battery of rarely performed tests on the feces extracted from the body and the true culprit was found.

Upon ingestion, 50% to 90% of polonium-210 will exit the body through the bowels via excrement. What remains in the body enters the bloodstream and travels to the spleen, kidneys, liver and bone marrow. To the inexperienced eye, radiation poisoning from polonium resembles end stage cancer.

Once G discovered the actual cause of Governor Gardner's death, all hell broke loose in the morgue, at the precinct, at the River House Restaurant and at the Governor's home. The U.S. Nuclear Regulatory Commission sent investigators to every location Governor Gardner had frequented in the months, weeks and days before his death. Everyone who had come in contact with the Governor… every item that he may have touched or that might have touched him was examined, reexamined and tested for contamination.

The only place traces of polonium were found was at the River House and only in the immediate area surrounding the table where the Governor had sat with his wife and friends. Nowhere else in the restaurant—not in the kitchen or storage areas, not on the pots, pans, dishes or utensils, not on the clothing of the wait staff or cooks—nowhere except in the approximately 36x36 inches allotted for a table of four was any trace of the deadly chemical element found. More specifically, the highest concentration was found in the Caesar salad and on the carpeting where Governor Gardner had expectorated upon dying.

Cat and Marci spent many hours with G discussing how the Governor could have swallowed a radioactive element that was occasionally used industrially and was only allowed to be sold under strict government control. Since large amounts of polonium could not be legally purchased, the only option would be to buy it on the black market from a weapons dealer specializing in chemical warfare.

"How would someone even get polonium into the country?" Marci was clearly fascinated by the choice of murder weapon and its method of conveyance to the United States.

"That's the easy part. Polonium can be transported as a crystal or in a powdered form. It can be diluted in a liquid… say, water… and it will not set off standard radiation detectors because it only emits alpha particles, and alpha particles aren't even strong enough to penetrate a piece of paper."

"But wouldn't the person carrying the polonium be in danger of dying?" Cat was also fascinated by the subject and, considering the turmoil in the world, thought that terrorists might have found an ingenious way to strike fear into the populace of every country they felt offended their faith.

"Well," G said, "if you are talking in terms of terrorism, the majority of them don't care about dying. They consider it a badge of honor. But, polonium only poses a problem to humans if it is ingested, breathed in, or absorbed through a cut or abrasion. If it is packed securely and only opened in a small space… if they never touch it with bare skin or inhale contaminated air, they are relatively safe."

"So an open wound can be the cause of death."

"Yes, Cat, that's a very viable means of entry into the human body just as it is for every disease and bacteria."

G was born to teach and, by sharing his knowledge with Cat and Marci, he guaranteed that the lessons learned from this case would be remembered and applied in the future should the need arise.

"That's fricking scary." Marci was sweating just thinking about the possible uses for the deadly poison.

"Yes, it is, and when you consider that an amount smaller than a single speck of pepper coming out of a grinder can cause death…"

A plausible answer to how Governor Gardner had died hung heavy in the air. Cat, Marci and G stared silently at each other for a half second. Then, Cat rose and went to the phone on G's desk. She dialed the number for the representative from the Nuclear Regulatory Commission who had been assigned to Governor Gardner's case after the polonium was discovered in his organs.

"This is Detective Jessica Leigh of the Palm Beach County Sheriff's Office. You need to collect all the pepper mills from the River House Restaurant and test them for radiation."

# CHAPTER EIGHTEEN

*S*ince Governor Gardner's death appeared to be an isolated incident, no one in law enforcement or local government considered the possibility of danger when the U.S. Conference of Mayors booked the West Palm Beach Convention Center for its annual gathering. The event was a huge affair which brought together top politicians from cities with populations of over 30,000 residents. There were nearly 1500 such cities in the country and each was represented at the conference by its highest elected official – the mayor.

If a threat assessment had been made prior to the commencement of the conference, it would have been determined that the attendees most in danger would be those sitting at the four tables closest to the kitchen in the main reception hall. Their water glasses were the first to be filled and their dinner plates were the last cleared away. A glance at the seating charge would have revealed that the young men and women at those tables were staff members of mayors from distant cities—San Francisco, California; Denver, Colorado; Olympia, Washington; Phoenix, and the once desert town now thriving city of Goodyear, both in Arizona. The tables were attended by three servers, each with a different and very specific responsibility.

Party Line, the events planning company responsible for handling every detail pertaining to the weekend affair, was highly regarded not just in Palm Beach County but on the entire eastern seaboard. They were a huge organization with teams in every major hub. The company did background searches on every person they hired, even part timers, which included fingerprinting, photographs, criminal records checks, a list of references and phone calls to past employers. Only those with a pristine work history were welcomed into the fold.

Before being assigned to an affair, new employees were put through a rigorous training program. They rehearsed with the same intensity as Broadway actors, staging and blocking larger parties so that one server never interfered with the responsibilities of another server. Watching the employees of Party Line work an event was like watching the Marine Corps Silent Drill Team perform on the White House lawn.

Party Line employees resembled military men and women in more than just their actions. They dressed identically in immaculate and perfectly pressed uniforms which included black dress pants, a white French-cuffed long sleeved shirt, simple gold cuff links, a matching two button jacket similar to a suit jacket but with extra room for ease of movement, and a black necktie subtly decorated with a few small gold crowns. Party Line's slogan was *The King of Quality,* and the company lived up to the motto in every way.

On their feet the wait staff wore black ABEO B.I.O. system shoes sold at The Walking Company. The shoes cost $159.00 a pair, but Party Line employees were well paid because management recognized that comfort was tantamount to good service.

The first hint of trouble began when a regular Party Line employee noticed a server on the floor not wearing the proper attire. Instead of the requisite formal jacket, shirt and pants, this man was dressed in black jeans, black vest, a wrinkled, short sleeved white shirt and a black bow tie that clipped onto his shirt collar. He was also wearing black sneakers, which gave him the appearance of a valet not a waiter. However, even valets hired by Party Line had a uniform, and it looked nothing like the ratty clothes this man was modeling.

The trained Party Line server took note that the intruder appeared not to know the company routine and continually bumped into or blocked the path of wait staff moving among the tables. With an event as large as this one, it was imperative that everyone be able to differentiate their left from their right, especially when serving and removing dishes at each place setting. Additionally, the man was carrying a plastic pitcher with which he used it to top off glasses that were already full. Party Line did not use plastic at upscale events.

With both anger and concern, the employee informed the catering manager that something was amiss. The catering manager was a man well-respected in the industry. He had begun with Party Line as a server eight years prior and had risen quickly to the highest local position available in the company. Although he no longer needed to physically work events, whenever something as important as the Conference of Mayors was in town, he was on site every minute of the day and night. He did not feel it was below him to work beside his staff, hustling dinners from the kitchen to the hungry guests awaiting their meals.

Notified of trouble in the ballroom, the catering manager hurried from the kitchen just as the man and another server got into a verbal confrontation. This server, who also realized something was wrong, was attempting to guide the man out of the reception area and into the kitchen without making a scene. The man refused to go and lifted the water pitcher as if to hit the server with it. The catering manager immediately intervened and was splashed with water as a result. The man became agitated and more aggressive, and the catering manager was forced to wrestle him to the ground. The water spilled onto the carpeting, but not before the man took a big gulp from the pitcher.

Captain Constantine saw the commotion and rushed to help while yelling for the security staff made up of off-duty police officers to offer assistance. Having seen the server drink from the pitcher, her highly tuned instincts left her with no doubts that she was watching a reenactment of the attack on Governor Gardner only on a much larger scale. As she ran across the ballroom floor, she intentionally knocked a glass of water from the hand of a woman about to take a sip. The only word she had time to say was, "Don't!"

Once the man was handcuffed and led out of the room, the guests were escorted to a second reception hall where they would be safe from contamination should Captain Constantine's gut prove to be correct. Everyone was told not to eat any of the food or drink any beverage that had already been placed on the table. Arrangements were made to bring in food from outside the Convention Center to fill the now loudly growling stomachs.

The first phone call Captain Constantine made was to G. He called the same representative from the U.S. Nuclear Regulatory Commission who had been an invaluable part of the Gardner investigation. The second was to the dispatcher at PBSO with a request that he contact her top detectives—Cat Leigh, Marci Welles, Moe Di Lorenzo and Norm Mack. All hands on deck was the only way to approach this investigation.

When Cat and Marci arrived at the Convention Center, it looked like an earthquake had hit downtown West Palm Beach. Men and women in hazmat suits rushed in and out of the building as if they were filming a scene from a sci-fi movie. Wearing protective clothing was a necessary extra precaution for anyone coming in direct contact with the still unidentified suspect currently handcuffed to a chair in an empty meeting room. Emergency vehicles of every make, model and size were parked haphazardly in the lot—some on the landscaped islands, others on the lawn and many on the sidewalks and pathways leading to the main entrance.

Cat and Marci left their car in a *No Parking Zone – Emergency Vehicles Only* spot on Okeechobee Boulevard about a half block from the Convention Center and trotted at a steady pace to the scene of the crime. Even without the *Officer On Duty* placard in the windshield, they would not have worried about being towed. Though unmarked, their late model sedan shouted cop so loudly it practically brought speeders to a standstill on the Interstate. Plus, neither of them could think of a bigger emergency than the potential poisoning and death of 300 people.

Making their way through the main lobby and up the escalator to the second floor was an Olympic-sized feat fit for a sumo wrestler. Shoulder force was needed to push media hounds who had snuck in through the underground passageways out of their path. Reporters, cameraman and lightening crews interfered with forward progress, causing even medical personnel to behave like professional football players during the Super Bowl.

When Cat and Marci finally arrived at the ballroom, Moe and Mack were waiting for them just outside the doors. Sheriff Brickshaw and Captain Constantine were a few feet away talking with FBI Special Agent in Charge Trevor Hoerler. When Hoerler saw Cat and Marci, he acknowledged them with a quick nod of his head and a barely discernible smile. Usually, contact between the FBI and local law enforcement agencies was limited, but since the PBSO detectives and the Miami Field Office agent had recently worked together on the Vincent Policastro murder, the resulting relationship was strong and respectful. Hoerler's presence made Cat and Marci feel more secure. The threat to national security was being taken seriously this time.

Cat, Marci, Moe and Mack split the job of interviewing guests and staff at the convention. They assigned uniformed officers to take down all names and contact information. Then, they had the guests and staff separated into those who were sitting and working at the back of the room closest to where the arrest took place. These people were put into another meeting room to wait while four separate interview areas were arranged. Those sitting at the front of the room, far away from the action, were allowed to leave once the investigators from the Nuclear Regulatory Commission were assured that they were safe from contamination both to themselves and the community. A number of hazmat-clad technicians, each with a portable gauge used to measure radioactivity, were moving from table to table testing the plates, glasses and utensils.

The catering manager and the suspect were quarantined in a

different part of the building as was the woman who had attempted to drink the water. All would be given preliminary examinations at the Convention Center before being sent to the hospital for further testing and treatment. Cat and Marci knew that the assassin accused of killing Alexander Litvinenko never actually touched the polonium and, yet, he was hospitalized for two weeks after carrying out his mission—much of that time at death's door.

The catering manager's exposure was limited to getting his clothes wet. No water appeared to have made contact with his eyes, nose or mouth. Thanks to the quick actions of Captain Constantine, who insisted he immediately remove his shirt after the fight with the suspect, and the fact that alpha particles cannot pass through the skin, he was expected to be fine. The thirsty female guest was also expected to suffer no ill consequences for her parched throat. Again, Captain Constantine's quick reflexes had saved a life.

The suspect, who was refusing to talk, had already been finger-printed and formal identification was, hopefully, just minutes away. He, too, would be sent to the hospital but, if he had ingested water contaminated with polonium as suspected, his chances of survival were nil. The length of time he had left depended upon the amount of the deadly chemical element in his system. Sooner or later, his internal organs would begin to shut down and death would result. Truth be told, a speck of polonium no bigger than the period at the end of a typed sentence was approximately 3,400 times the lethal dose for human beings, and a single gulp of water would far surpass that amount.

Under normal circumstances, investigators would need to follow the radioactive trail polonium leaves on everything it touches in order to find a viable suspect. Since polonium had a short life—approxi-mately 138 days before half of a given quantity began to decay—they would need to work fast. The pseudo waiter had made that step unnec-essary as had an examination of the water in the pitcher and on the floor. Polonium was definitely present.

Even though an autopsy would be done upon the death of the suspect, it was a foregone conclusion that polonium would prove to be the cause. G knew, as did the NRC investigators, that should the suspect linger longer than 50 days, his body would automatically begin to eliminate half of whatever amount of polonium-210 had been ingested. Knowing what they already knew, that fact would be irrelevant. The suspect would be lucky to have five days left to live.

Seeing G hard at work directing his technicians in the collection of evidence, Cat stopped to ask a quick question. "Is there any chance the suspect will survive?"

"Not a one, Detective. There is no cure for radiation poisoning and, if the amount we think he ingested is correct, his time is very limited. It could be a matter of weeks, days, hours or minutes. You need to interrogate him asap."

"Did you happen to take a picture of him before he was dragged off by the Feds?"

G raised his plastic glove wrapped hand in a "Yes. Of course," salute and pointed to his iPad, which was laying on a nearby table. Marci hit the start button and immediately the face of Brandon Hanson filled the screen. He was smiling his usual bewildered smile.

"Well, speak of the devil." Marci held the iPad up for Cat to see. A *We've got you now* look passed quickly over Cat's face.

With a quick "Thank you" to G, Cat and Marci set out to meet Brandon Hanson in person. Now that Governor Gardner's presumed killer was in custody, it was just a matter of finding out why someone as unlikely as Hanson had chosen to murder so many people, and whether anyone else was involved. Piece of cake… or not.

Formal identification of the suspect via fingerprints was received within the hour but since Brandon Hanson was still quarantined and being examined by doctors from the NRC, Cat and Marci decided to start their investigation by talking with the waiter who had originally reported him to the catering manager.

"The guy was walking around with a pitcher, adding more water to already filled glasses. I asked him what he was doing and he said, 'What I was told to do.' I knew he hadn't been told to do something that had already been done. What an asshole."

Since that was the extent of the contact between the two men, and since no other staff members had had any interaction with the suspect, Cat and Marci left Moe and Mack to finish up at the Convention Center. After being cleared through the NRC quarantine zone, they got in their car and headed over to Brandon Hanson's house.

# CHAPTER NINETEEN

$\mathcal{H}$ome for Brandon Hanson was his parents' 2600 square foot Key West style ranch in a Palm Beach Gardens gated community. His apartment was a converted two car garage that had been made into a combination bedroom/living room/office. The garage was just a few steps from the kitchen and guest bathroom in the main house, accessible from the connecting laundry room. When hungry or in need of using the facilities, Hanson would leave his man cave. Other than that, he rarely communicated with his mother and father. He entered and exited his personal space by means of the electric garage door, which functioned as one wall of the apartment.

Although a loner by choice, he did manage to support himself with a variety of jobs. He had worked as a dishwasher and busboy in several local restaurants, which explained why he was familiar with the process of serving tables. Real friends were few and far between but he had hundreds of acquaintances on social media—people he met on the numerous trips he took. Hanson was a restless man, unable to stay in one place for too long. By saving his pennies and with a little help from his parents, he was able to take cruises or fly off at minute's notice when the urge struck him. Cat and Marci got the impression that his parents were glad to be rid of him so money was readily available.

Through conversations with his parents, the detectives learned that Brandon had had big dreams. For a few years in his early twenties, he tried and failed to support himself as a stand-up comic in Los Angeles. His stage name was Sputnik—an apt choice for someone whose reality was out of this world most of the time. His career was short lived as almost every club manager told him, "You scare the patrons. Don't come back."

In person, Brandon was an interesting human specimen in more ways than one. A pudgy, rosy-faced man in his early forties, he had a receding hairline which encircled a mass of unruly curls in the center of his head. His outward demeanor was best described as soft, meaning someone more likely to be bullied than to do the bullying. He kept his voice low and calm when he spoke. He giggled easily and when he did, his entire body took part in the joke. Confused might be an accurate first impression, but aggressive or angry... never.

Brandon fancied himself a writer. He was a frequent attendee at the Santa Barbara Writers Conference, where he rarely contributed any work but was always ready to comment on the narratives of other authors. He took copious notes at these events and used them to start but never finish hundreds of stories and screenplays. He erratically attended a writing class held at a local acting school in Jupiter, Florida, and the instructor of that class told Cat and Marci that, had Brandon been able to harness his thoughts into a cohesive narrative, he would have been brilliant.

"Amid all the cubic zirconias he brought to class, there were, occasionally, Hope diamonds. I was quite fond of him. He had such a sweet soul." the teacher offered as a critique of Brandon's writing abilities and personality.

When Cat and Marci searched Brandon's apartment, they found the bookshelves filled with a library's worth of hard copy novels and paperbacks. The spaces between the paragraphs and around the edges of each page were filled with random thoughts that Brandon wrote in stream of consciousness style. Interestingly enough, the bookends holding all those volumes upright were wooden pepper mills. The Nuclear Regulatory Commission was quickly called.

The Hanson family home was quarantined and Mr. and Dr. Hanson were checked for signs of radiation poisoning. They were clean. The only place a small signature was found was in Brandon's room. None of the pepper mills showed signs of being used to season Governor Gardner's Caesar salad with polonium. Investigators did find sales receipts from a company in New Mexico that legally sold very minute quantities of polonium-210 for $69.00.

The website for United Nuclear used up a lot of space emphasizing and re-emphasizing the fact that none of the radioactive materials they sold were hazardous. Bob Lazar, physicist and owner of United Nuclear, had gone on record saying, "The amount of polonium-210, as well as any of the isotopes we sell, is an exempt quantity. These quantities of radioactive material are not hazardous which is why they are permitted by the Nuclear Regulatory Commission to be sold to the general public without any sort of license."

The NRC confirmed Lazar's statement under questioning from Cat and Marci, who refused to be distracted by the familiar *ask a question in answer to a question* technique of avoiding answering a question. The detectives and G, who they later told of their findings, were shocked to learn that a deadly poison was available by mail order.

Upon questioning by Cat and Marci, Dr. Hanson proved to be surprisingly open to answering questions about her son. Perhaps, too open. If ever there was any doubt that psychiatrists could benefit from a little *physician heal thyself* therapy, Dr. Hanson was proof positive. Brandon Hanson was strange. Dr. Hanson was stranger.

"When my son was still a child, around eight years old, I diagnosed him as having multiple personality disorder. The more familiar term these days is dissociative personality disorder. The symptoms were most severe when he was young—between the ages of five and 13. At that time, he had seven different people living inside his mind and body. Over the years, I've been able to exorcise four of them, but the remaining three—well, actually two, because one is the real Brandon—have been very difficult to remove."

"Difficult?" Cat pushed for clarification. Marci was unable to speak. Her pen was still poised over the notebook she carried, frozen in mid air when she heard the number "seven" bandied about.

"They have become firmly implanted in Brandon's psyche... a natural extension of his personality. I'll try to explain by starting at the beginning. When Brandon was very young, he was deeply attached to his paternal grandfather. Brandon has attention deficit/hyperactivity disorder—ADHD. The only person who could control his rambunc-tiousness was my father- in-law. For some reason, Brandon could sit for hours with him and just listen to the stories he told. My father-in-law was far from the nicest person in the world, but where Brandon was concerned, he had tons of patience. He never spoke to Brandon the way most adults speak to a child. He forced Brandon to understand the world in adult terms, and Brandon seemed to thrive on being treated as an equal.

My father-in-law passed away suddenly when Brandon was five, and shortly thereafter, the personalities began to emerge. The first was a perfect representation of my father-in-law. Brandon would sit in his room holding a picture of his grandfather and have a two-way conver-sation. He accurately mimicked my father-in-law's voice and, using the photo as his physical likeness, he would talk for hours about every-thing and anything.

In the beginning, it gave my husband and me the creeps, but once we realized those conversations had the effect of keeping Brandon calm, we encouraged him to continue. Now, in hindsight, that may have been a mistake."

"How long did the grandfather personality last?"

"Oh, it's on going. There are times I would honestly like to elimi-nate the other two and keep grandpa, but that wouldn't be fair to Brandon."

"Tell me about the other personalities. Were any of them trouble-some?" Marci was writing furiously so Cat continued asking the questions.

"Not early on. Many of them were quite appealing. There was a very short-lived one named Nomad, who claimed he was a clown with the Ringling Brothers Circus. Nomad only lasted four days. As I'm sure you know, Ringling Brothers is a traveling circus so Nomad only stayed as long as the circus was in town.

There was a traveling preacher—I can't remember his name—but Brandon was deeply attached to him. He came from some imaginary place—a planet, I think, called Nirvana or Nevada—Nev something. The preacher's mission was to spread a message of positivity in the world. Brandon has always been a very kind soul. He hates it when people are intentionally mean to one another. He was so intent on making the world a better place that for a while he would haunt the local radio stations, trying either to get a job as a host or to get interviewed on the shows. They thought he was crazy. He was finally banned from entering the buildings.

When Brandon was in his twenties, Peter Pierpont began surfacing. He was, according to his Brandon, a Parisian trained gourmet chef. Quite a blessing he was to have in the kitchen after a long day with patients. I rather enjoyed all the fancy meals he cooked."

"I imagine you did."

"It was so interesting, Detective Leigh, to watch Peter while he created his signature dishes. As a child, Brandon wouldn't so much as peel a banana for himself. Peter, however, would buy whole, fresh fish and gut and clean them. He would buy freshly killed chickens from local farmers and take pleasure in singeing whatever feathers remained off their bodies. Brandon, as Peter, was almost perfect. I regretted having to force him out of the family so to speak."

"And why did you have to do that?"

"Well, whenever Peter needed to mix a salad dressing or a marinade, he would put the ingredients—oil, vinegar, lemon juice, spices like oregano and garlic, whatever he chose to use—into his mouth and swish them around. Then, he would spit the liquid out onto whatever he was making before refrigerating it. He claimed saliva helped the flavors adhere to the food. It was most unappetizing to watch and even less appealing to eat."

"Okay, now!" Marci, who was known for having a sensitive stomach when it came to certain foods, found her voice. "Moving on. At what point did Brandon make the threat against FAU?"

"It wasn't a real threat, Detective. Brandon was just trying to make a point."

"And what point would that be?" Marci held her pen in the air as though directing an orchestra.

"That good people should be rewarded and bad people should be punished. I know how that sounds, but Brandon felt that a grown man didn't have time to waste. Changing the world could take years. He chose words that he felt could not be ignored."

"He, obviously, got his teacher's attention. The man called security in fear of his life."

"Brandon was never aggressive. When detained by the security officer at the university, he was non-confrontational. Never once did he exhibit signs of violence."

"But he talked about killing people. No matter how you think to do that, even if it is with kindness, it is threatening." Cat kept her own voice low and conversational in tone.

"It wasn't Brandon's message that was threatening. It was the way he chose to deliver it that frightened people"

Cat brought the discussion back to Brandon's most recent *other* selves. "Tell us about Brandon's current personalities."

"It's only recently that one of the personalities has become problematic. He doesn't have a name or, if he does, he hasn't been willing to tell me. This person is very different from all the others. He's angry. Vengeful. There is hate in him."

Marci's interest was piqued. "Any idea why this sudden change in disposition?"

"Well, Brandon was fired from a job he loved about a year ago. That's when I first noticed that a dark cloud seemed to have settled over him. For some reason, the new personality had a southern accent. I asked him once where he was from and he told me Little Rock, Arkansas. Brandon's never been to Arkansas so I thought that was strange."

"Yeah... not ever having been in Arkansas is definitely the strange part." Marci went back to taking notes.

"This man, whoever he was, would tell me stories about murders he'd committed. He saw himself as a vigilante. There was a politician he supposedly shot in 2008 because his gun policies would benefit criminals. Brandon believed that the politician was plotting to overthrow the government and that he was targeting Brandon for telling the truth.

Another time Brandon claimed he had murdered two prosecutors in Texas because they had successfully defended some skinheads... sorry, members of the Aryan Brotherhood... and gained their acquittal on charges of having tortured a black man. He said he killed these men in the fight for racial equality.

He also claimed to have slit the throat of a strip club owner who refused to pay his girls for performing sex acts on the customers. Brandon... or whoever he was at the time... said that the owner of the club forced the girls into prostitution and then beat them if they demanded to be paid. I actually read a news report about a similar incident and the police had the killer in custody, so I think Brando was just projecting onto stories he read or heard. There were others but I would have to go back through my notes."

"Why do you think Brandon became obsessed with these stories?"

"He needed to feel like a hero." Dr. Hanson smiled at the detectives like a proud mother.

By the time Cat and Marci left to interview Brandon Hanson face to face, they were beyond curious about their suspect.

By his own admission, Brandon Hanson was a confused man. "Masculine. Feminine. Fate's devious plot. Who is it I am? Who is it I'm not?"

Without ever being asked anything about his sexual preferences, Brandon told Cat and Marci that he did not know whether he was gay or straight. He stressed that he was a virgin but not by choice. He wanted, craved actually, a sexual relationship with someone. He just didn't know whether that someone was male or female.

As the interview went on, Cat and Marci realized they did not need a medical degree to recognize that Brandon was already showing signs of radiation poisoning. His physical discomfort, however, had little to do with his decidedly unbalanced mental state. He repeatedly claimed to have e.s.p. and attempted to torment Cat by pelting her with verbal reminders of her assault at the hands of Bobby Bridgeman.

"I'm sorry you're in pain, Detective Leigh."

"What are you talking about?" Cat's body language spoke volumes. She was suspicious, nervous, curious but, mostly, angry.

"What Bobby did to you was unforgivable. May I see your tattoo?"

"I don't have a tattoo."

"Yes, you do."

"You're awfully sure of yourself."

"I know lots of things people don't expect me to know."

"Tell me."

"I know that Bobby always chose pretty women with long hair. He was good at making ponytails, wasn't he? Please. Can't I see your tattoo?"

"How do you know so much about Robert Bridgeman?"

"I know Bobby named his victims after the color of the ribbons he put in their hair. I know that he tattooed their names on his back. His back was his trophy wall."

"That's all common knowledge… reported by the media during and after the Ribbon Rapist case." Marci moved between Cat and Brandon as if proximity could protect her best friend and partner from the verbal assault she was taking.

"I know he tattooed your name… Miss Blue… on his back because he thought he was going to kill you. But, he didn't, and now you're here asking me about Governor Gardner. Funny how fate brought us all together."

"Fate has nothing to do with us being here. You killed someone and tried to kill many more. Everything you know was reported by the media. You're no mind reader." Marci's internal barometer was rising.

"Brandon, how do you know about my tattoo?" Cat's voice was low and encouraging. "That's never been in the papers, and I'm careful never to show it in photographs."

"I told you. I have e.s.p. I know you have a teal blue survivor ribbon on your left wrist."

"There is no such thing as e.s.p. Tell me the truth. How do you know about my tattoo?"

"The same way I know you are in pain, but it isn't physical pain. You hurt in your heart because you still haven't found the bodies of Miss Orange and Miss Purple. Bobby told me."

"Bobby is dead. The dead don't talk and, even if they did, he wouldn't know about the tattoo." Cat struggled to remain in control of her emotions but impatience was being to show in the way she spoke her words.

"The dead know everything. They talk to me. I guess you could say they're my confidential informants."

"Cute. Now, let's get back to your attempt to commit multiple murders at the Mayors' Conference." Marci was seething and growing angry with Brandon's attempt at brain games.

Cat, however, wasn't ready to move on. She put her hand on Marci's shoulder in a manner that said, "Not yet. I need to know more." Marci took a few steps back and allowed Cat to continue with the questioning.

"Brandon, you are a very clever man and, I have to admit, you've got me curious. What else have the dead told you about me?"

"I know what you told your family when you got the tattoo. 'Since I have to remember what happened for the rest of my life, I want to remember that I survived.'"

Cat stared at Marci, her eyes telegraphing "how the hell does he know these things?"

Silently, the detectives communicated their indecision as to which path to follow in this interrogation. Should they walk through the Ribbon Rapist door that Brandon Hanson had opened or follow the polonium trail that had led them to his hospital room? Was there a chance the two were connected?

Cat made the decision for both herself and Marci. "As I said, you are a very clever man, but we're not here to talk about me, although we may revisit that line of questioning in the future. For now, let's talk about you and why you killed Governor Gardner and then tried to murder a room full of innocent people."

"Very well, Detective Leigh. If that is what you wish. Just don't wait too long to ask me... well, actually, to ask Bobby... where those poor ladies are buried. Polonium works rather quickly. I would hate for you to lose the chance to bring peace to their families... and yourself."

"You're full of shit, Hanson. Let's cut the crap." Marci was furious that Brandon continued to taunt Cat about the one case that haunted her dreams. Every detective had, at least, one. For Cat, it was the Ribbon Rapist.

With a shrug of his shoulders, Brandon began talking incessantly about a television series he wanted to produce... one that would deliver uplifting messages to the world. It was impossible for Cat and Marci to control the conversation so they let him ramble. From under the blanket that covered his body, he pulled a plastic bag filled with letters he had received from famous people in response to letters he had sent to them. By his own estimate, he had written over 1,000 letters. He had no idea that the responses he got were form letters sent by staff members whose only job was to stamp a signature onto a photograph or note and send it back.

"There's a note here from Clint Eastwood. He wrote that my letter "... made his day.""

One of the most telling parts of the interrogation was when Brandon Hanson admitted to wanting to blow up the School of Communications at FAU. He firmly believed that if he could get the attention of the media, the world would listen to and embrace his message of positivity.

"I did and I didn't want to blow up the school. What I really wanted was to force them to see things my way. I wanted to leave them no option but to change. Unfortunately, that isn't how life works. Threats are useless. Actions do speak louder than words."

Marci used this admission to segue into a discussion of recent events. She began with his arrest at the Convention Center.

"Brandon," Marci started the questioning, "why did you want to poison all the people at the Mayors' Conference?"

"I didn't... not all of them. Not any of them really, but how else could I get the world's attention?"

"What did you want the world to know?"

"People are suffering. They need a lifeline to cling to. The media has a responsibility to listeners to give them something better than scare tactics. Fear might be a good marketing tool to get viewers, but it isn't right to plant ideas that aren't true in people's heads."

"Has someone planted ideas in your head?" Cat was fascinated by what she was hearing.

"The spirits of the dead call to me. There was a time when I couldn't hear the voices... when I could shut them out... but not anymore. Sometimes I feel like they are driving through my mind in a race car leaving skid mark messages on my soul. I used to tell myself to just wait and they would go away, but they never did."

"What do the spirits say to you?"

"When I was younger, they told me that I was a failure. They said I would never be good enough so no one would love me. I tried to convince myself that I wasn't the person the voices said I was. Sometimes, I succeeded, but never for long. I was a prisoner of all the negative vibrations fed into my brain."

"And it's because of those messages that you are trying to change the world?"

"Yes. I realized that if I wanted to be free of them, I would have to change the radio waves over which the broadcast was sent. That's why I wanted a job at a radio station... so I could spread my message worldwide."

"But no one would hire you."

"They thought I was nuts. They laughed at me. But I know I'm right. I know that people are tired of the malicious words and images they are forced to see and hear every day. People are angry. They want to be surrounded by goodwill and kindness... by people who care. Charity and generosity are never going to go out of style, but right now it seems those qualities have been pushed into the back of a closet. You know... the way we push aside clothes we don't wear anymore. We pile all kinds of junk on top of them. People need inspiration. They need hope, and I had hoped to give it to them."

"By killing people?"

"Politicians aren't people. They are the problem, not the solution."

"Some of the people you could have killed weren't politicians. They were just staff members... people working a job in order to pay their bills. People like you."

"Not like me. We all make choices. If you share the beliefs of a monster... if you choose to feed yourself by dining at the side of that monster, then you have to suffer the consequences when that monster is put down."

"Was Governor Gardner a monster?"

"I had no idea a governor was eating at the restaurant that night. I didn't and still don't know anything about him. He just happened to be in the wrong place at the wrong time. Well, wrong for him. Perfect for me. The River House was a trial run to see if I could get away with eliminating someone in a restaurant. I was pretty sure I could. No one really notices their server. No one ever noticed me."

"What's the difference between eliminating someone and murdering someone?"

"Eliminating means to defeat an enemy... like in football when the teams eliminate their rivals from competition."

"And murder?"

"You are a homicide detective, right?"

Cat ignored Brandon's sarcasm. "What made you choose the River House?"

"I used to work there as a busboy. It was a long time ago. Every day was like my first day. No one ever remembered my name so I knew no one would remember my face. The patio is accessible from the garden. It's so easy to get into the main dining room. I just dressed in my old uniform and acted like I belonged."

"How did you administer the poison?"

"You already know. My mother told me you confiscated all the pepper mills in my room. Pretty ingenious, don't you think?"

"None of those pepper mills were radioactive. What did you do with the one you used."

"Please, Detective Leigh, let me keep, at least, one secret."

"Why polonium?"

"It's the perfect poison, so perfect that spies use it to knock off their enemies. Governments use it for sanctioned kills. It's odorless. Tasteless. Easily transported and so rare that it isn't a part of standard toxicology screens."

"You're very well informed."

"I read a lot. You saw all my books. And the internet... it's like having a library in your bedroom. Plus, I get guidance from another dimension."

"Polonium is almost impossible to buy."

"Almost being the definitive word. Everything is for sale these days, Detective Leigh, if you know where to look."

CHAPTER TWENTY

*B*y the time Cat and Marci completed their interrogation of Brandon Hansom, they no longer knew with whom they had been speaking. His demeanor had gone from the shy, unpresuming man first introduced to them to someone with an inherent inclination toward evil. Maybe the dead did talk and Bobby Bridgeman had taken over Brandon's body. That was an area the detectives planed to investigate once their reports on the Gardner case were filed. Unfortunately, twenty four hours after leaving Brandon at the hospital, he was dead. Any questions that still required answers would remain that way.

Cat's and Marci's written and oral reports to Captain Constantine were filled with observations, perceptions and assessments that would become text book training material and seminar topics in the years to come. At present, they made for interesting dinner conversations shared by police officers in Florida and throughout the country. Law enforcement agencies worldwide were smart enough to know that if one person could figure out how to buy deadly amounts of polonium, many more would follow.

"Remember all the legitimate deals we were offered to turn the Kalendar Killer case into a book and movie?" Marci saw dollar signs floating over her head every time she thought about the case that had put them in the spotlight a few years earlier. "We turned them down and somebody went and made the movie anyway. Well, I think the Polonium Killer is going to bring more offers our way."

"We didn't accept the deals then and we won't now." Cat yawned her response.

"Maybe we should think twice about that. Why should other people get rich on our hard work?"

"Well, for one thing, our contracts say we can't monetize our cases for personal gain. The big boys in Tallahassee would come down hard on us."

"So what? We'd be rich. We wouldn't need to work anymore. We'd never again have to attend any high society tea parties where we are pranced around like prized horses."

"Just call me grateful that the case is over." Cat picked up the murder book she had been working on and headed toward the conference room. "You coming? Moe and Mack are waiting for us."

Prior to closing an investigation, it was standard procedure for all involved officers to review the details and sign off on the case file. Before dying, Brandon Hanson had provided a lot of much needed information. While he did take certain pertinent details to his grave— like the location of the pepper mill used at the River House Restaurant —Cat, Marci, Moe and Mack accepted that miracles weren't a part of their job descriptions. Since none of them were able to talk to the dead, they were left with no other choice than to move on.

"I'm still having a hard time knowing that our elected officials have allowed companies like that place in New Mexico to sell dangerous substances to the public. I really don't care that the amount is small. They're still selling poison." Moe's frustration with what he called "governing by collusion" was well known.

"Do you know what the greatest sin is in our society? It's that we condone human behavior as it is rather than as it should be."

"That's very philosophical, Mack. And true. Society has become accepting of a lot of bad behavior. There doesn't seem to be any punishment… and I use that word loosely… for acting in a manner my mother calls "uncivilized." Now, people just think they can say and do whatever they want without consequences. I guess that's why companies like United Nuclear don't care that they could be including death sentences along with their sales to the crazies of this world."

Everyone at the table knew that Marci was thinking of Sonora Leslie and the kind of world the little girl would be inheriting from her parents.

"I'm less worried about what is being sold by United Nuclear than I am with what Brian Boucher found available on the dark web. What the hell is the dark web anyway." Norm Mack was just as frustrated as his partner.

Marci sat up straighter in her chair. This was a topic she had researched and, with the help of Brian Boucher, the internet specialist who had helped capture the Kalendar Killers, she was now very well informed.

"There are three methods to search the internet: the surface web, the deep web and the dark web. The surface web can access all information that is available to a regular search engine like Google, Yahoo, Bing, Firefox, and all the rest.

The deep web looks for information those search engines can't find. You can't access the deep web just by typing in a question because it doesn't use links the way the surface net does. It uses search boxes. The deep web isn't illegal or scary the way the media wants you to believe, but it does require more knowledge than the average person surfacing the internet.

Now, the dark web is another story. The dark web is a small portion of the deep web that has been intentionally hidden and is inaccessible to web browsers like Google et al. You need specific proxy software or authentication to gain access. If you are accessing a site that deals in illegal activities—like the sale of polonium—you usually have to give before you get. In other words, to guarantee your silence, you have to provide information that can be used against you should you try to do those sites harm."

"Fascinating," Mack commented, "but what could Brandon Hanson give the dark web that could be used against him?"

"Proof that he committed murder, I suspect." Cat had gone over these questions in her head a million times. She had one of her own that was especially gnawing.

"How much does it cost to buy enough polonium to kill 300 people? The United Nuclear website states that a person would need to place 15,000 orders costing more than $1 million before they would have enough polonium to hurt someone. Do any of us believe, even for a second, that the dark web is giving polonium away at bargain prices? Brandon Hanson was a busboy. He lived with his parents.

Yes, his mother and father had money but not that kind of money. How did he buy polonium? There is a lot more to this case than we know, and I fear we will never have all the answers, which could lead to more of the same trouble in the future. I'd give anything to find that damned pepper mill. My gut tells me other people... maybe lots of other people... are involved."

"Are you suggesting that a foreign government is behind this?" Marci asked.

"I'm not suggesting anything. I'm just throwing out questions and hoping that an answer will drop down out of the air. Polonium is a byproduct of nuclear reactors. It decays quickly so to have it available for sale on the internet, there needs to be a viable source. Which countries with nuclear capabilities would benefit from selling polonium to our enemies?

I believe that Brandon Hanson was a means to an end, not the source from which the evil flowed. I have a terrible feeling that while we are closing out this case, our investigation has only started."

"What's most important is not what you hear; it's what you observe." Marci's words caused Cat to stare at her partner, a perplexed look on her face.

"That's a very astute observation. I don't recall Sherlock Holmes ever saying it."

"That's because he didn't. Harry Bosch said it... well, actually

Michael Connolly wrote it in *Trunk Music*. It stuck with me when I read the book."

As a somber mood settled over the conference room, the four detectives signed off on the Hanson and Gardner cases. On their way back to their office, Cat and Marci were hailed by Captain Constantine, who was waving a case folder over her head.

～

"I guess there really is no rest for the weary, Cat. The Hanson investigation took a lot out of me. I was hoping we'd get some breathing room before our next case." Marci nibbled at her cuticles while she expressed her frustration to Cat.

"Take your fingers out of your mouth. I hardly saw you do that at all the last few months. Why start now?"

"I chew when I'm challenged and right now, I'm being challenged to rethink my career path. Do you know what it's like to go home at night, hold Sonora Leslie in my arms, and worry about whether or not some screwball is filling the drinking fountains at the park with polonium or some such crap?"

"And, what? Ignorance would be bliss. At least, you're in a position to do something about those screwballs should they cross your path."

Marci picked a piece of cuticle from her tongue and flicked it into the air while watching Cat out of the corner or her eye. She saw her partner cringe and smiled.

"I've missed your lectures. I promise I will not bite my fingers any more… at least, not where you can see me."

"Terrific. Now, open the file and tell me where we are going."

～

The entrance to the Jupiter Beach Resort and Spa was at the intersection of Indiantown Road and A1A North. It was built along 1,000 feet of pristine Atlantic shoreline. The hotel's 168 rooms were decorated with an island flair that was tasteful, warm, and welcoming. Guests had the choice of dining casually at The Sandbar or in the more sophisticated atmosphere of Sinclair's. Both restaurants offered a varied menu with seating just footsteps from the ocean's roar.

The resort was a popular destination year round but, for families and singles needing a break from northern winters, it was paradise among the palm trees. Ideally situated at the northern end of Palm Beach County, the Jupiter Beach Resort allowed easy access to West Palm Beach's popular night spots, while providing the illusion of a secluded oasis. In March and April, the rooms were filled with young men and women who no longer craved the wild parties synonymous with spring break but who still desired a bit of adventure in their sun and surf escapes. Should an evening interlude with an attractive member of the opposite sex be presented, the unspoken agreement was *what happens in Florida stays in Florida.*

Five obviously nervous men were sitting in the hotel lobby under the watchful eye of a uniformed officer when Cat and Marci arrived. The detectives estimated their ages to be between 28 and 30 years of age and, from the way they leaned into each in an attempt to keep their conversation private, they appeared to know each other well. They had, as Cat and Marci would soon learn, been college classmates and roommates at Fordham University. At this moment, those carefree years seemed to have taken place a lifetime ago.

Graduation and job searches had put thousands of physical miles between the men, but their friendships stayed strong. Every year they took one week from their busy schedules to meet somewhere warm... somewhere where they could reconnect, reminisce and recreate those fun days when everything seemed possible. While adventure was always a part of their vacation plans, never did they expect to be suspects in the murder of a woman they barely knew.

After introductions were made, the men began to talk over one another, trying to tell their stories before any questions were asked. Cat brought everyone in line.

"First of all, gentlemen, you can relax. You are not at this time suspected of any wrong doing. Your morals might be in question but not your culpability. My partner and I merely want to ask you some questions. We need to know how you are connected to Melissa Miller and whether, perhaps without realizing it, you are in possession of information that could explain why she turned up dead in a motel on Dixie Highway."

"I guess I knew her best." Rod Osmond was the youngest member of the group. He was also the best looking. Whenever the friends traveled together, it was his job to attract likely "contestants" for their game of *Who can get laid the most.*

"I met Haley... Melissa... here in the lobby the first day we arrived. She came in from the pool, stopped at the sundries shop, and we bumped into each other at the checkout counter. We started talking. She said she lived locally but liked to come to the hotel to get away from it all from time to time. I asked if she was alone and she said she was."

"So, she was a guest at the hotel?" Marci led the questioning.

"I thought she was but, later, it turned out she wasn't."

"Explain, please."

"Well, one thing led to another and we went to my room for a quickie. We had fun. She was really sweet. After she left, I realized I hadn't gotten her room number. I went down to the lobby and asked for her at the desk. They told me no one by the name of Haley was registered, and no one recognized her from the picture I had taken with my cell phone. The desk clerk just shrugged his shoulders."

"Where were the rest of you while Rod was entertaining Melissa in his room?" Cat joined the conversation.

"At the pool." Joshua Presley, the old man of the group, looked to his friends for agreement as he answered Cat's question. At 40, Presley was considered the father figure... the one who was supposed to keep everybody else from making a mistake they would regret for the rest of their lives. On this trip, he had failed to fulfill his job requirements.

"Okay, Rod. What did you do when you couldn't find Melissa."

"I went back to my room, changed into my bathing trunks and joined the guys at the pool. It wasn't until hours later that I found she had left a phone number written on one of the hotel postcards. It was on the desk.

I thought the whole situation was weird so I threw the card in the waste basket. Then, I took it out and put it in my wallet. I don't know why. I can't explain it even now."

According to their statements, the five pals spent the next two days on the beach and enjoying the nightlife on Clematis Street. They had "a great time." It wasn't until Rick asked Rod what he had done with Haley's phone number that, according to Rod, he "... even remembered her. I pulled the post card out of my pocket. Guess I had a little too much to drink because I called her. This is where it gets really strange."

The story continued under Cat's and Marci's probing questions. Rod explained that a woman answered the phone. He asked for Haley and the woman asked who was calling. He told her and she said that she was Haley but her real name was Melissa. She invited Rod and the guys over to her house.

"Like I said," Rod qualified his actions, "we were a little drunk so we stupidly decided to go."

"What happened when you got there?"

"More weirdness," Rick answered sheepishly. "We sat in the living room drinking beer. Everything was cool. Just conversation about everyday stuff. The phone rang in the kitchen and Melissa got up to answer it. We could hear her conversation. She said, 'They're here. Come on over.'"

By this time, the men were jacked from all the drinking. They claimed they thought Melissa had invited some girlfriends to join them, but when she came back to the living room, she was acting strangely. According to Rick, "She seemed nervous... like she was up to something no good."

Josh picked up the story at this point. "I had to pee so I went to the bathroom which was down a hallway and out of sight. On my way back, I saw some envelopes on a table. I don't know why I stopped to look at her mail, but when I saw that all the envelopes were addressed to different people, I got worried. Some of the envelopes were addressed to a Mr. and Mrs. Landers. None of them were addressed to Melissa or Haley.

I brought the mail back to the living room. Melissa was in the kitchen getting more beers. We decided to get out of there. We just up and left. There were too many bad vibes."

"And that was the last time you saw her?" Marci was writing furiously in her notebook.

"Yes and no," Rod brought the story to a conclusion. "The next day, out of curiosity, we drove past the house. A little girl, maybe five years old, was playing in the front yard while a man and woman were taking suitcases out of the trunk of a car. The kid called the woman 'Mommy.' She wasn't Melissa."

Cat stood up to indicate that the meeting was over for the moment. "We'll need the address of that house. Don't leave town, gentlemen. No doubt, we will have more questions for you in the next few days."

"Our vacation is over tomorrow. We're scheduled to fly home in the afternoon."

"Change your plans."

The body of Melissa Miller, or what was left of it, was found in a room at one of the 20 and 10 motels on Dixie Highway in West Palm Beach. The term referred to the hourly cost for a room ($10.00) and the average price for a hooker. Since the body on the bed had been decapitated, the police were initially unaware of the woman's identity. Fingerprints gave the victim a name and a long list of arrests gave the police a possible motive.

Melissa Miller was the property of D'Shawn Williams, a known drug dealer and pimp. Williams not only sold; he used, and when he was high, he was notorious for beating his girls to within an inch of their lives. For Melissa Miller, the thin line between life and death had been crossed.

Born into poverty, Melissa was adopted by a well-to-do family. Her upbringing was about as atypical for a prostitute as someone could get. She attended private grammar and high schools where she was an honor roll student. College would not be a financial burden as her grade point average guaranteed that scholarships would be plentiful. Her future looked bright, and Harvard appeared to be high on her list of preferred universities. With her college entrance exam scores at the highest levels, her admission seemed a done deal. She also had ethnicity on her side.

Melissa Miller was black. Her parents were white. Given up for adoption by a crack addicted mother, she never asked about her parentage. She had no interest in knowing who her real mother and father had been. She lived in a beautiful home, had beautiful clothes, drove a nice car and had lots of friends. Her parents took her on vacations and paid for her to take music and dance lessons. Her mother and father adored her and she adored them. Life was good... until her senior year of high school. That was when she met D'Shawn Williams at West Palm Beach's annual Sunfest celebration.

Williams was handsome, strong and a bit of a rebel. He complimented Melissa and tempted her with visions of celebrity. "You could be a model. I know someone who could help you get into the business." Melissa felt excitement course through her veins. She fell in love and life as she had known it came to an end.

The move away from the security and safety of her parents' house was gradual. First, she started staying out past curfew. Although she did graduate high school, she never completed the forms required for admission into college. She quit her part time job. Eventually, she stopped coming home at all. Her parents tried everything. They threatened to send her away to a military boot camp. They bribed her with a trip to Europe... a year living anywhere she wanted before beginning her university studies. They begged and pleaded and cried. Nothing worked.

By the time Melissa was found dead at the age of 21, she looked decades older. She was no longer recognizable to her parents as the little girl to whom they had given their hearts. The needle marks between her toes and the bruises on her body had brought her back to her roots. Birth mother and daughter had not only come into life the same way; they had exited the same way.

There was never any doubt that D'Shawn Williams had killed Melissa Miller. His DNA and fingerprints were recovered from numerous surfaces in the motel room. The *why* was another matter as was the location of Melissa's head. Finding Williams should have been easy. He was known to frequent most of the Lake Worth low-life bars and hangouts popular with MLK gang members, and his home address was on file with the courts. Either he had packed up and moved away very quickly or he was in deep hiding because he had become a ghost around town. No amount of pounding the pavements or pounding the faces of his posse turned up any clues to his whereabouts.

The only reason Rod Osmond, Jonathan Presley and their three pals were part of the PBSO investigation was because Melissa's cell phone was found under the motel room bed. The photo Rod had taken of her was on it. The view from the balcony where she had posed was of the ocean, the mangroves and two flags flapping in the breeze. One was Old Glory. The other bore the name and logo of the Jupiter Beach Resort and Spa.

The house where the college buddies had shared beers with Melissa Miller was owned by Douglas and Victoria Landers. They had a six-year-old daughter named Kimberly. The Landers had lived in the Magnolia Bay subdivision for ten years. They were well-known and well-liked for being community involved.

A review of police calls confirmed that they had filed a report of a break in at their home while they were on vacation. While the house had not been destroyed in the burglary, electronics and jewelry were missing. Food and alcohol were also taken from the refrigerator and pantry. Investigators confirmed that the back door had been opened with a bump key. None of the neighbors noticed anything strange or, if they had, no one was willing to admit that they had been too busy caring about themselves to worry about their friends. How Melissa and D'Shawn knew that the Landers were away was a mystery still waiting to be solved.

Once Cat and Marci confirmed that Rod Osmond and his pals were only peripherally involved with Melissa Miller's murder, they were allowed to go home. Since all their contact information was on file, they would be notified if and when a court appearance was required. That would only happen after D'Shawn Williams was found and indicted. The detectives were hoping that Melissa's head would be included in their discovery. In the meantime, Rod Osmond, who was married, needed to decide if and when he would tell his wife about his escapade in sunny Florida.

# CHAPTER TWENTY-ONE

*O*n the Tuesday after a long holiday weekend, Marci arrived at
the office earlier than usual. She had had trouble sleeping—a
feeling that something major was about to happen keeping her awake
all night. Rather than stare into the dark, she showered, dressed, kissed
a sleeping Ian and Sonora Leslie goodbye and headed out. The bullpen
was empty when she arrived. She made coffee and, hot cup in hand,
she walked slowly to the office she shared with Cat.

As she sat at her desk, she pulled the wire basket with the open
unsolved folders into the middle of her blotter as was her daily routine.
She held her hands, palms together, above the one remaining file and
began to rub them together. The phone rang.

G's very nasal, very irritating yet very funny imitation of Jerry
Lewis came through the receiver.

"Hey. Hey. Detective Lady. I've got something here you and Cat
will want to see."

Cat had also had a restless night. It was not unusual for the partners
to share premonitions. She, too, had chosen to shower, dress, kiss her
sleeping husband goodbye and head for the precinct before the sun
came up.

Having seen Marci's car in the parking lot, Cat knew hot coffee would be waiting. She stopped to fill her thermal cup and then made her way to the office. No soon had she stepped through the doorway than Marci motioned for her to turn around and head back out.

Hearing Marci tell G, "We're on our way," was enough to have Cat backpedaling out the door.

On their way to the Coroner's Office, Cat and Marci discussed possibilities. It wasn't like G to waste their time. If he requested their presence in the morgue, especially at this early hour, it had to be important. It also wasn't like G, who was the most conscientious medical examiner ever to hold court in the world of the dead, to be waiting for them in the reception area. He stopped pacing only long enough to say, "Good morning," and usher them into his secret lair.

"Two bodies were brought in during the night. That's not unusual. Actually, getting just two bodies after a holiday weekend is rare. Usually, the hallways are stacked with celebration accidentals and intentionals. It's amazing how many murders are committed on what are supposed to be happy occasions."

"What makes what you are going to show us so special, G?" The nervous energy Cat was feeling was evident in her voice.

"Tell me, Marci," G asked, "… did you rub your hands over the last open unsolved file in your basket this morning?"

"I did. Actually was doing that when you called. Why?"

"You'll see. Follow me."

Cat's and Marci's obsession with finding the last two victims of the Ribbon Rapist was well known throughout Florida law enforcement. PBSO, FDLE and local police forces all knew to keep their eyes open for anything that might help them find Miss Orange and Miss Purple. Three years had passed since Cat killed Robert Bridgeman on the front porch of her house. If not for the tattoos on his shoulder listing the nicknames he gave his victims, Cat and Marci would not have been aware that there were other women waiting for someone to find them. The trail had grown not just cold but frigid. Still, Cat held out hope that the victims and their families would one day have closure.

"Yesterday, the police in Lake Worth were canvassing for a missing person in an area of abandoned houses." G led Cat and Marci into the autopsy suite as he spoke. "They entered one particularly dilapidated residence and were overwhelmed with the foul odor of decaying human remains. A homeless man had died – natural causes, nothing suspicious – and, of course, no one had missed him. In doing a routine search of the premises, the officers made an interesting discovery.

In the garage, an old chest freezer—the kind you can slip a padlock through to keep it secured—was still plugged in and running. For some reason, Florida Power and Light had never shut off the electricity to the garage... only to the main house. One of the cops broke the lock and opened the top expecting nothing more than some badly frost bitten packages of hamburger meat. He found a body. A woman with purple ribbons in her hair."

"And you didn't call us immediately?" Cat didn't know whether to be angry or ecstatic.

"I wasn't informed until this morning. Lake Worth thought it was a new case. It wasn't until they ran a missing persons search that they realized the body might be connected to the Ribbon Rapist."

"Where is the body now?" Cat was pacing like a caged tiger.

"Here. I will be doing the autopsy shortly. However, there is something else, and this is why I asked Marci if she had rubbed her hands together this morning."

"You're killing us, G," Marci said. "Just give us the whole scoop."

"Last night officers in Delray Beach chased a car thief for over an hour through the streets of the city. Eventually, the chase took them into a wooded, swampy no trespass area near the intersection of Lyons Road and Atlantic Avenue. The guy they were chasing slammed into an old black pickup truck that was caught in the muddy field. The truck had also been stolen and was probably abandoned there by whoever took it."

"And?" Marci was growing agitated.

"Be patient, Detective. All this information is valuable to you and your case. The truck had a covered bed. Once the officers handcuffed the man they were chasing, they decided to take a cursory look under the truck bed cover just so they could complete their report. They, too, found a body. They called for detectives from the Violent Crimes Division and, upon arriving at the scene, those detectives immediately thought of your case. I believe we have found Miss Orange."

"Holy shit!" Cat and Marci spoke in unison. "What proof do you have?"

"I will do both autopsies today but I am already certain your last two victims have been found. The body in the truck was badly decomposed, but a member of the crime scene unit found a small piece of orange ribbon tangled in her hair. I don't know if we will be able to make a formal identification of either woman since they may not be in any data bases, but at least they will be treated with dignity in these last few days before they are buried."

One week later Cat and Marci attended two funerals. Distant relatives of the victims had been notified and claimed the bodies. The families of Denise Chambers (Miss Orange) and Josie Hall (Miss Purple) held services in their respective churches.

Formal identifications had been made after G was able to extract DNA from the hair samples taken from Josie Hall. Sheer luck had pointed him in the direction of an ancestry testing lab where he learned that Josie had been searching her past in the hope of finding long lost relatives. Providing a DNA sample was part of the protocol for an in depth search.

Denise Chambers' fingerprints were on file as the result of a background check done when she applied for a government job some years ago. Both women had been only children whose parents had died a long time ago.

Whether their solo status in the world had been the reason they were chosen by Robert Bridgeman would never be known. Neither would anyone ever know how the women had come in contact with Bridgeman. Cat and Marci had to be content that they had fulfilled their promise to bring their bodies home. In the end, all they could do was kneel and bow their heads in a final goodbye.

# CHAPTER TWENTY-TWO

*D*espite their hectic schedules and family obligations, Cat and Marci continued to speak to advocacy groups and professional organizations about security issues facing women in an increasingly dangerous world. On a Thursday afternoon of an especially busy week, the detectives took their places on stage and waited to be introduced by the moderator of the South Florida Women's Resource Center. The topic for the afternoon was *Women Empowering Women.*

"Ladies and gentlemen, it is my pleasure to introduce two individuals who have made protecting our community, women in particular, a high priority in their personal lives and careers. I'm sure their names will be familiar to you. Palm Beach County Sheriff's Office Homicide Detectives Jessica Leigh and Marcassy Welles are not strangers to publicity. They are responsible for the capture of the Kalendar Killers who terrorized Palm Beach County a few years ago, and for the demise of Robert Bridgeman, known in the press as the Ribbon Rapist. Detective Leigh was herself a victim of Mr. Bridgeman and her insights into what women… and men… need to do to stay safe come from a deeply personal experience.

Without further ado, I give you Detective Jessica Leigh."

Cat stepped to the podium and looked into the attentive eyes of her audience. Her first thoughts before beginning a speech were always whether or not her words would generate an attack from people who felt she was finger pointing... blaming women for being victims. Taking a pre-emptive approach, she was well prepared this afternoon.

"Good afternoon. If you read the Wikipedia page dedicated to bull dogs, you will understand why I consider myself a kindred spirit. Bulldogs are normally docile and happy to please. Although low to the ground, they can move quickly when the need arises. Occasionally, they can be willful and stubborn.

That's me. No matter how troubled I am in my personal life, I try always to smile and spare others the misery loves company routine. Like that little bull dog, I can run – especially my mouth off. Get me started on topics dealing with women's rights, and I'll talk until your ears bleed. Injustice gnaws away at my insides and, like a bull dog, I'm ready to fight whenever the need arises.

Rarely am I stumped when formulating a battle plan. I'm good with words and my favorite weapon is to use insightful commentary that forces the listener to consider all sides to an issue, especially when it comes to violent crime... anatomy specific assault in particular.

Recently, I sent a letter to our local newspaper in which I discussed the need for women to take responsibility for their own safety. The letter was one of many I've sent on the same topic since my rape at the hands of Robert Bridgeman. Very few of them have been printed. My message is not one that the liberal media embraces because it requires that common sense always be a part of our safety equation and, as we all know, common sense isn't really very common.

Frustration forced me to demand a reason from the editor for why letters such as mine — written by women who have known the pain of rape — are ignored."

Cat picked up a wireless presenter and pointed it at the projection screen to her right. On that screen was a printout of the emails Cat had exchanged with the editor of the opinion page at the Palm Beach Post. She asked the audience to follow along as she read their exchanges.

In her first email, Cat asked the editor to honestly answer why it was that *whenever* a woman wrote an article encouraging other women, especially those who had been raped, to disclose their identities and take a stand by fighting back through the courts or in the legislature, no paper was willing to publish it.

Cat had pointedly asked the editor, "Is it your goal to treat us as victims forever? Is being a survivor not something to celebrate?"

The editor's response to Cat was short and reminiscent of a politician who had years before questioned the meaning of the word "is."

"You say "whenever." What is that based on?

The communications continued with Cat explaining that she had submitted articles on this topic to many media outlets, including the Post, and that she rarely got a response.

"Every time I write an article that attempts to move rape out of the realm of sex crime and into its deserved place as a violent crime, the press turns a deaf ear. Every survivor I've ever met agrees that until we can speak about rape openly and honestly, we'll never reduce the assault rate. Until that day, rapists will always have the advantage."

The editor's response was again terse. "I can't speak for *other media outlets*. I'd say the Post has given you room for comment."

Cat explained to the audience that the Post had, indeed, printed a few of her letters and that she appreciated what space they had given her. She also said that her final email to the editor, in which she said, "To make change, one must make waves. The media, the Post, in particular, seems to like still water."

The only response she received was silence.

"That was the end of our conversation. The dialogue—if it ever was a dialogue—ended abruptly. Notice that I never did get an answer to my original question. Thanks to this editor, I now know what is meant by 'a man of few words.'

Truthfully, I don't care how often my letters and editorials wind up in a circular file. I don't care how many rejection notices I receive.

Being ignored has never stopped me. As long as women are in

danger of being assaulted, I will keep writing and speaking. As long as women like you attend these meetings, I will preach from my soapbox until I've whittled it down to a pile of toothpicks. Then, I will stack those toothpicks one on top of the other and keep talking. I encourage you to do the same.

I cannot tell you how often I have heard survivors say, "If pursuing my attacker in a court of law spares even only one more woman from being raped, then everything I went through was worth it."

Survivors mean exactly that. They would gladly relive the pain and trauma again IF they knew that other women would learn from their experiences. After all, we're talking about saving lives and when is saving lives not worth every effort we can make?

I'm going to sit down before you get tired of hearing my voice and allow my partner and best friend, Detective Marci Welles, to take the stage. Then, hopefully, we will continue this discussion. Thank you."

Cat sat to the sound of loud applause. Marci smiled her encouragement as she made her way to the podium.

"Good afternoon. As Cat has already mentioned, my name is Marci Welles and she and I have investigated murders committed in Palm Beach County for many years. We were best friends in high school and our friendship has grown stronger each day that we have been partners in the Homicide Division of the Palm Beach County Sheriff's Office. Together we have made it our goal to keep women safe by speaking the truth about violent crime and the need to take personal responsibility for our own safety.

I am a huge fan of the television series *Blue Bloods* starring Tom Selleck as Police Commission Frank Reagan, and it isn't just because I think Selleck is one hot hunk. I like the show because it applauds family values and encourages open and honest discussion between family members on topics that are relevant to all of us. The show is in some ways a throwback to the 1950s when the family was all important and morals and values were taught at the dinner table.

A few years ago, the show aired an episode entitled *Power of the Press*. I've never forgotten it. Part of the story focused on the prevalence of date rape cases on college campuses and the reluctance of universities to pursue perpetrators in a court of law. That's a very relevant topic these days when more and more young women are being subjected to assault by fellow classmates.

Although the scenario depicted in the *Power of the Press* episode was typical of most scripts written to shine a light on rape, there was one line of dialogue which echoed something Cat and I have been preaching for some time now and which most advocates do not stress often enough in their efforts to eliminate this horrific crime.

I'm going to assume you all know the cast of this series, but if you don't, I'd like to introduce you to them. "Meet the Reagan family."

Marci pointed the wireless presenter at the projection screen and the faces of Tom Selleck, Donnie Wahlberg, Bridget Moynahan, Will Estes, Len Cariou, Amy Carlson and Sami Gayle filled the screen.

"In the episode I mentioned, Assistant District Attorney Erin Reagan..." Marci aimed the presenter at the face of Bridge Moynahan, "... is successful in her efforts to arrest the fictional Hudson University's Dean of Students for withholding evidence in a date rape case.

She takes this opportunity to discuss the dangers of excessive drinking with her own daughter, Nicky, a soon-to-be college freshman." The red light on the presenter moved to the face of Sami Gale.

"More specifically, she explained the need to be vigilant in choosing friends in an atmosphere of new freedom giddiness and release from parental supervision. She stressed that as a prosecutor, she had seen the devastation rape causes survivors and their families, and she advised her daughter never to relinquish control of herself to a bottle or a person unknown.

Of course, teenage daughter Nicky rolled her eyes, as teenagers are wont to do, and assured her mother that she already knew all the facts. She claimed she had heard them often over the years. Reagan's... Moynahan's face told a different story but it was her words – ten simple but powerful words – that brought the message home: 'The only one who can keep you safe is you.'

I have lost track of how many times Cat and I have told an audience that while it is true that women can go where they want, behave as they want and wear what they want, it is also true that they should not do so without considering the possible outcome. Drinking to oblivion is an invitation to assault. How many more young women need to suffer the horrible consequences of this fact before we start speaking the truth?

Rape is wrong no matter the circumstances. The victim is never responsible for the attack. Women should have the same freedoms as men, but we don't. It's time to face reality. We are not equal to men when it comes to protecting ourselves. We are vulnerable.

Responsibility is not gender-specific. Women are not excused from acting sensibly. In fact, by virtue of their smaller, weaker stature, women of every age must be hyper-vigilant. If we are to remain safe, we must both respect and protect ourselves.

The school bell is about to ring and while mothers of pre-teen students are busy filling backpacks with notebooks, pencils, markers and assorted necessities, mothers of college-aged girls are also preparing to pack bags. For parents of young women heading off to schools of higher education the sight of suitcases in the hallway can be traumatic. Yes, tuition is a frightening reality—one that could play havoc with your savings account for many years. Eventually, though, the bills will be paid and your daughters will begin earning their own way in the world. That's a good thing.

Unfortunately, there is another frightening reality—one which many parents refuse to accept—mothers, in particular. Whenever Cat and I speak to individuals and groups about the need for all women regardless of their age to take responsibility for their own safety, it is inevitably the mothers of daughters in the last years of high school or about to enter college who balk at the suggestion. They seem to resent being advised that their daughters need to be careful about the who, where and how of enjoying themselves.

Taking responsibility does not mean denying oneself a good time.

It doesn't mean you cannot party with your friends or drink or dress provocatively. It does, however, mean that the good times will not be marred by painful memories in years to come.

If I had a penny, even as worthless as pennies have become, for every time we have heard "rite of passage," Cat and I would be very wealthy. I always think that people are confusing *rite* with *right* because although you do have the *right* to go, dress and behave as you choose, the *rite* that you may be participating in could be rape. Here is where we get the most flack.

Invariably, there will be one mother who will spout the line about how what you wear has no correlation to rape... and that is true to a certain degree. Rapists aren't necessarily drawn to sexy attire unless that attire will make it hard for the intended victim to get away. Just try running in five-inch heels. See how far you get. Consider that being unconscious in a pool of vomit, whether wearing a designer dress or a suit of armor, is not only unattractive, it's also an open invitation to every pervert lurking nearby.

College is a transitional period for all students. Both males and females get their first taste of freedom and, more often than not, they are unprepared for the dangers inherent in the absence of parental supervision. Despite what some factions would like you to believe, not all men are potential rapists. However, there are rapists in college just as there are everywhere in life. Date rape is a controversial subject which I will not address here. My comments are generalizations meant to keep all women safe throughout their lives.

No woman deserves to be raped. Choosing to go naked through the streets does not qualify a female as being rape worthy. Nothing a woman does... no manner of behavior... justifies abuse. However, if you are going to dress provocatively, if you are going to drink to excess, if you are going to habituate areas that are less than safe, you had best be aware that the fact that you don't deserve to be raped means nothing to a rapist.

Women should able to do as they please without fear of assault, but we don't exist between the pages of a story book where the princess lives happily ever after. This is real life and here the princess can wake up brutally beaten—as did happen to Cat—if she is lucky enough to wake up at all. Why? Because she chose to protect herself with rhetoric rather than reason.

Don't be a victim. Don't allow your daughters to be victims. Talk to your children about the danger in acting irresponsibly. Mottos and slogans can't save your life, but here's one that might detour you and your family out of harm's way: "Think before you drink." Let's make that motto even simpler—"Just think." And don't expect someone else to protect you. If you do, the results could be devastating.

Before your daughters head off to college... before you head out for an evening on the town... consider heeding one very savvy scripts writers words. No one and nothing can protect you from danger as well as you can do it yourself. Safety cannot be legislated. Rapists don't care about your constitutional rights. Mottos and slogans won't save your life. Awareness will. Think first. Act second.

Thank you. Now, Cat is going to bring this afternoon to a close with a few last words."

"Thank you, Marci. The human anatomy is an interesting body of work. Held together by muscles and tendons, we come in many shapes and sizes, varying colors and distinguishing facial features. Some of us have blond hair, some brunette, and others auburn or raven tresses. Some of us even come by those colors naturally.

Our eyes are very often our most distinguishing feature, and the more vivid the color, the more likely someone will remember us. If we are tall, we stand out in the crowd. Short -- we take the chance of being trampled. Marci will confirm that statement.

Full lips, big breasts, tiny waist, firm butt, long legs— these are all things people talk about without the slightest hesitation. Considering that conversations in which these topics arise are often sexist, it amazes me how little controversy they cause.

My father was a doctor. I worked in his office when I was still a teenager. Not one patient ever squirmed when hearing about hernias, ulcers, bladder infections, menstruation or childbirth. Body functions were discussed openly and without discomfort. Over lunches and dinners with friends in the medical field, my parents would discuss every aspect of the human form and no one blushed.

When it came time to teach me about life and sex, my parents did so honestly. They never allowed cutesy words to substitute for the actual appendage we were discussing. Arms were arms. Legs were legs. Breasts were breasts. The male and female genitalia were named appropriately. As a result, I grew up without any embarrassment about my body. That's actually something that makes me quite proud.

Thanks to the current *no holds barred* approach to television advertising common these days, people have grown accustomed to hearing about stomach ailments, urinary incontinence, diarrhea and even erectile dysfunction. Tell me why then does the mere use of the word penis send the media diving for cover.

Here we have a five letter word—doesn't take up much space on the page or anywhere else for that matter—but if a writer, in particular, a reporter, dares to use it, they are almost guaranteed that their work will never be seen. Conversely, if a writer wants to get attention, all he or she has to do is use the "F" bomb and it's a national headline.

Until we better educate society... until we can talk openly about human sexuality... rape survivors will continue to shiver in the shadows. When it comes to rape and anatomy specific assault, a penis is a weapon—nothing more!

Say it aloud! Repeat it over and over again! A penis is just a weapon—nothing more. We must remove the stigma of shame associated with rape. Only then will rape take its rightful place as a violent crime—not a sex crime—and rapists finally be treated like the vicious predators they are.

By the way, if this is the first time you are hearing me speak on this issue, anatomy specific assault is my preferred way of discussing what the media and the legal system call sexual assault. Please stop using that term. Until we do, nothing will change. Those three letters —S. E. X—guarantee lots of attention but for the wrong reasons.

Don't allow the status quo to reign. Don't accept rhetoric over reason. Be a catalyst for change. Women should make the rules for those matters that affect them personally and nothing is more personal than rape.

Before I bid you adieu, I'd like to share with you some of the letters I've received from men and women across the country and even abroad. These individuals have either attended events where Marci and I have spoken or they have read something I've written about my experience and my thoughts on rape. I will only refer to these people by their initials as I have not asked for permission to use their names."

The projection screen sprung to life as Cat aimed the presenter in its direction. She read excerpts from the letters she had received to the audience.

"From Mr. B.A.: Detective Leigh, as a defense lawyer with some 36 years of experience, I have concluded that it is impossible to have a rational discussion on rape in the abstract. I will only say that the counsel to young women that you advocate as a practical matter makes perfect sense to me.

From Ms. F.A.: I've been following your ordeal ever since it made the newspapers. I admire your advocacy for rape victims and your common sense approach to avoiding rape. I live my life by always choosing reason over rhetoric as a general rule.

From Mrs. R: A sad but true reality is that far too many people, especially women, view taking personal responsibility for themselves as *making excuses* for the choices made by others. There is a faction of society which says that because I stayed with my abusive husband for 12 years that I *deserved* what happened to me. My personal view is that, had I never gotten involved with him in the first damn place, he would never have abused me or my children. Thus, I am responsible for the decision to marry him but I am not responsible for his decision to abuse. Acknowledging that, had I made a different decision to start with things would have turned out differently, is not the same thing as saying that I deserved to be abused. Anyone who says that they are the same thing is being as manipulative as the abuser himself.

Mrs. R's letter is a perfect example of how society's thinking can be manipulated by those with nefarious motives. It has always fascinated me that women who have known the trauma of rape and abuse have less need to yell about what's fair than those who have not suffered that pain.

Men who commit rape choose to do it for a variety of reasons. Usually, physical proximity and opportunity are enough. We all need to understand that taking personal responsibility for our own safety means accepting that we must always be aware of our vulnerabilities and our surroundings.

I would like to close with this letter I received from Ms. L.H. Again, the projection screen lit up.

From Ms. L.H.: I'd like to live in a world where I'm always safe but I live in the real world. I don't leave doors or windows unlocked. At night I keep the windows closed in the bedrooms if I'm sitting in the living room. I don't walk through dark parking lots alone. Instead, I bother someone to walk me to my car. I read somewhere that you said, 'Until we make victim a word to fear in the hearts of all criminals -- rapists, murderers, thieves... all criminals -- nothing will change.' That's one of the most beautiful things I've ever read. I long for the day when people understand that truth."

Cat ended her commentary by adding, "Needless to say, I also long for that day. Thank you."

When the auditorium had emptied and only Cat and Marci were left, Marci smiled her approval at Cat for having the courage to speak the truth. "You do like to rock the boat, my friend."

Cat's response, "Grrrrr!"

# EPILOGUE

*I*t was a common occurrence to see river otters splashing and swimming in the canal behind the PBSO Headquarters on Gun Club Road in West Palm Beach. When not eating, which occupied a great deal of their time, the otters would amuse themselves with games of chase the stick, hide and seek and roll in the grass. These pastimes were accompanied by chirps, barks, whistles, grunts, squeals and growls... the equivalent of human laughter.

Watching these sweet-faced members of the weasel family interact with one another was a popular way for PBSO officers and staff to spend their lunch hours and smoking breaks. During the period from February to April, the canal banks were especially congested with human visitors as this was when the female otters gave birth. Within two months, the little ones were strong enough to join their adult family members in the water and the sight of them was something special to see.

While otters were not known for being aggressive toward humans, there had been a number of attacks on people reported in recent months, the latest on a 90-year-old man who was taking his morning constitutional around his retirement community. The potentially rabid otter came streaking out of the bushes near the man-made canals that dotted the community's landscape and bit the man's sandal-clad foot, causing him to fall to the ground. In defending himself from the possessed animal, the elderly gentleman sustained serious injuries to his hands and feet.

Regardless of the potential for danger, the noon time show at the PBSO water-side picnic area was well attended each day by men and women who found the acrobatic otters' antics cause for choruses of "Oh's" and "Ah's." So popular were the aquatic acrobats that people began researching them and sharing the information with their co-workers. A game of *Who Knew?* was all the rage, with one department trying to outdo another with quirky facts about their unofficial mascots. One of the most interesting facts to surface was that otters quite fear-lessly attacked alligators when they were hungry.

In the majority of places that otters called home, they were consid-ered the most voracious predators—even in those places where alliga-tors shared the land and the water. It was not unusual for a male otter to attack a three or four-year-old gator. Since, at four years of age, an alli-gator would already be five feet long and weigh approximately 15 pounds and since the otter would have a maximum weight of 30 pounds… well, the otter was nothing if not daring.

Occasionally, an alligator would be sighted in the canal on Gun Club Road where the otters lived and played. Not wanting anything to happen to their furry friends or to the alligator, PBSO had an under-standing with Fish and Wildlife to have the unwanted visitor removed asap. It was this potential for survival of the fittest that gave Officer Keith McKinney an opportunity to pay back Detectives Moe Di Lorenzo and Norm Mack for their "Play dumb" comment during the investigation into the murder of Gamalial Cohen.

Without exception, each of the brothers in blue had fallen victim to some wry comment or practical joke played by the detectives with whom they worked. The uniformed officers were bound by brotherly loyalty to exact revenge by plotting a joke of their own.

So it was on a dark and dreary Monday morning after an especially homicide heavy weekend that Moe and Mack found themselves leaving headquarters with the sun just peeking over the horizon. The parking lot was cast in shadow. Their unmarked vehicle, barely illuminated by an overhead streetlight, looked like a gigantic saucer-eyed frog waiting to pounce.

Too tired to pay much attention to their surroundings, the partners made their way to their vehicle in silence. Moe was a few steps behind Mack as he was busy texting his wife that he was finally coming home. It wasn't until he reached for the car handle that he saw the unexpected visitor crawling out from under the vehicle. His screams broke the silence of the pre-dawn morning.

The head of an enormous alligator, dead otter held between its powerful jaws, beady eyes glowing ominously as it stared at Moe's frozen face was only a heartbeat away. Moe's initial scream had been silenced by the drumbeat in his chest. He dropped his cell phone and began to pray.

Mack came running from the driver's side of the car. He, too, started screaming, but his screams were curses shouted at the top of his lungs.

"Son of a bitch! Mother fucker! Comer mierda! Fanculo! Help!! Help!!"

"Leave it to a cop to be able to curse in every language." Mack recovered enough to push his partner out of the path of the alligator.

Both men quickly backed away from the car. Moe struggled to lift his overly wide backside onto the hood of the adjacently parked car. Mack pulled his gun and pointed it at the gator. He stared, unable to pull the trigger, his mouth hanging open in surprise and awe. The alligator continued to stare back... but it didn't move. Mack took a firing stance.

"Shoot him! Shoot him, Mack. What are you waiting for?" Moe sounded ready to cry.

Just then, a familiar voice awakened them from their terror stricken poses.

"Ah, guys, don't tell me you're afraid of a little old alligator. He's not interested in you. See. He's already got his meal for the day."

Keith McKinney walked up behind Mack, stepped over to the alligator, bend down and patted its head. "Good hunting, fella."

No longer able to control themselves, McKinney and about a dozen officers, including Cat, Marci and Captain Constantine, who had been hiding in the shadows, began to laugh uncontrollably.

"Who's the dumb one now, Moe?" McKinney asked, a *gotcha* smile on his face as he picked up the humongous reptile and walked away.

~

"That was probably the best $20.00 I've ever spent." Cat yawned as she and Marci made their way to their respective cars, intending to head home after a long night. "Any time McKinney needs to rent a truck to transport an alligator to headquarters, I'm in."

"Yeah," Marci yawned back, "if we had to work the night shift, I can't think of a better way for it to end. Who knew that his father was a taxidermist? I sure didn't."

"Me, either, but I'm glad he was and that he was willing to let Keith borrow Mr. Magnificent for a few hours."

"Mr. Magnificent... weird name for an alligator."

"In case you didn't notice, he was nearly ten feet long and probably weighed, when alive, between 400 and 500 pounds. I'd say that's pretty damned magnificent."

"Hey, do you know what they call an alligator wearing a vest?" Cat was already laughing at what she considered a funny joke.

"I don't know," Marci humored her friend and partner.

"An investigator."

"Cute, but I've got a better one." Even after a long night of gore and guts, Marci was ready for a contest of one-upmanship. "What do you call a criminal defense attorney?"

"I'll bite." Cat giggled with weariness.

"A litigator."

"And that's why alligators don't attack lawyers. Professional courtesy." Cat and Marci high-fived each other.

"Ba boom ditty boom! Good night, Cat."

"Night, Marci. Drive safe."

Keith McKinney and a few brothers in blue were loading Mr. Magnificent into a truck as Cat and Marci drove out of the parking lot. The alligator had served his purpose and now it was time for him to go home, too.

Moe and Mack were back in the office, soothing their wounded egos with donuts and stale coffee. Although they would never give Officer Keith McKinney the satisfaction of knowing just how effective his joke had been, both detectives agreed that Mr. Magnificent had nearly scared the shit out of them... literally.

# TOTAL SUBMISSION

## THE THIRD CAT LEIGH AND MARCI WELLES CRIME NOVEL

### PROLOGUE

*T*he sound of a metal file drawer slamming shut woke Cat from her reverie; Marci's loud muttering forcing her to shake the cobwebs from her brain.

"Some days suck. They just suck."

Once Marci's words sank in, Cat nodded in agreement. The partners had just closed an emotionally difficult case… emotional because it involved one of their own. A divorced police officer with two teenage daughters had been murdered by his girlfriend after a misguided attempt on her part to get a marriage proposal. She tried to make her cop boyfriend jealous by claiming that she was pregnant with another man's child. She even went so far as to buy a maternity shirt with fake belly at a costume store.

The woman contrived an intricate tale in which she blamed the pregnancy on her boyfriend in blue. Claiming that she was depressed and feeling unloved by his refusal to tie the knot, she had found solace in an affair. The soon-to-be baby was the result.

The cop, thinking he knew the identity of his girlfriend's lover, rushed out of the house in a fit of rage. He found the man in a neighborhood biker bar. An argument ensued. The cop shot the man – who was innocent of any wrongdoing - killing him. In the confusion that followed, he escaped.

Unaware that the supposed lover was not guilty, the boyfriend returned home intent on doing God knows what to his girlfriend. Only after she heard what had happened did she take off her shirt and show him her flat stomach. The cop, now on the brink of insanity, tried to strangle her.

The girlfriend grabbed his gun and shot him twice... the first shot hit him just below the armpit; the second hit his jugular vein. Thinking he was dead, she wrapped him in a blanket, took his cell phone and car keys and left the house. The cop quickly bled out.

At trial, the girlfriend was found guilty of second-degree murder and sentenced to 20 years in prison. Two men had lost their lives; two high school girls were left without a father; a family had been destroyed; the law enforcement community was feeling a sense of desolation and *til death do us part* had taken on a whole new meaning.

"Whatta ya say? Want to hit the gym before we go home. I feel like pummeling someone and a punching bag would be a safer alternative."

Cat heard the tension in Marci's voice and realized she was feeling much the same way. Side by side, the partners headed for the elevator.

# CHAPTER ONE

"I like sex. Not as much as I like Mallomars, but I like it."

*H* omicide Detective Jessica "Cat" Leigh chuckled as she gave her best friend and partner, Marcassy "Marci" Welles, a push through the double steel doors that marked the entrance to what they called *hell on earth*. The women had known each other since their student days at Wellington High School, and the bond they shared was envied by many of their colleagues at the Palm Beach County Sheriff's Office. Not even hell... or Marci's penchant for chocolate... could come between them.

"You can laugh all you want, Cat, but it's a proven fact that chocolate is addictive. Scientists studied rats that were fed nothing but junk food and determined that cupcakes and cookies have the same effect on the brain as cocaine -- the release of dopamine D2 receptors."

"Dopamine?"

"Yeah. It's the chemical that's released when you're exercising or having sex."

"That's good to know."

"You're missing the point. Sex is an exercise. And since sex produces dopamine, that makes intercourse addictive. Thus, if I eat Mallomars while having sex, I won't have to go to the gym as often."

Cat gave Marci another push... this one a little bit harder than the first.

As the heavy steel doors slammed shut behind the ladies, the moans and groans that filled the dungeon-like chamber took on a rhythmic, almost musical, quality. Each guttural note was preceded by the percussion of leather on flesh. There was a sensual... sexual... overtone to the sounds that, when mingled with the odor of perspiration, signaled the release of physical tension and emotional satisfaction. The concrete walls and floors were silent witnesses to the many bodies that writhed in agony and bliss as one master held sway over their rewards and punishments.

Tres Douloureux, a 3,000 square foot facility where only the most hardcore gym rats – those who desired physical perfection – were allowed entry, was ruled over by trainer and world weightlifting champion Terrance Sandefur. This vast open space of gray painted cinder block walls was not a place for the average health nut who thought running ten miles on a treadmill made them a superstar. Here serious training took place geared for those who put their lives on the line every day.

TD was not open to the general public. There were no memberships offering special deals if you signed up *today* – no free 7-day VIP passes, no short term contracts, no day care services. Only two types of people were allowed inside its hallowed halls – military men and women and law enforcement officers.

Sandefur put his minions through extremely strenuous workouts designed to break them if not make them into human fighting machines. One of the toughest routines, called The Complex, required trainees to move from one exercise to another while carrying a 44 lb. Olympic bar. Each exercise was performed three times for a total of 30 repetitions. It was a killer... almost literally.

Three times a week Cat and Marci challenged themselves by attempting to complete their specially designed strength training program -- 50 reps each in box jumps, jumping pull-ups, kettle swings, walking lunges, knees to elbows, push presses, back extensions, wall ball shots, burpees and double unders. They also spent endless hours learning the art of bob and weave and the finer points of kick boxing. Knowing that regular physical exercise was tantamount to maintaining memory, concentration, and mental sharpness, Cat and Marci were fervent disciples of Sandefur and his "... better sore than sorry" philosophy.

Every Monday, Wednesday and Friday while the sky was still chalkboard black, the partners drove through the silent streets of West Palm Beach to reach the darkened doors of their chosen place of worship. The gym was their church -- each squat, punch and lift a prayer. Whether in the boxing ring, in the weight room or on the floor mats, they were fervent in their dedication to Sandefur and his methods. After nine years, the women had reached a level that many of their male colleagues envied.

Envy was an emotion Cat and Marci understood well. Not that they were envious of others. This was a case of others being somewhat envious of them. Envious and scared. The partners were known for their ability to communicate with each other without speaking, and that capability had given rise to the belief that they could read minds. Their male counterparts at the PBSO were hesitant to think anything but the cleanest of thoughts when Cat and Marci were nearby. When alone, the ladies enjoyed many a chuckle over their feigned superpowers.

On this particular Monday morning, Cat proved her competence in the boxing ring by holding her own against a much larger, male opponent. Marci, on the floor mats a few feet away, held her leg raised in a perfectly executed roundhouse kick -- not an easy feat for someone whose center of gravity was low to the ground. Whereas Cat was nearly 6 feet tall, Marci was best described as petite - a term she despised but preferred to the teasingly whispered "midget" used by her peers at the Sheriff's Office. After 45 minutes of strenuous training, the women were having difficulty breathing, but on their faces was a look of determination that dared anyone to get in their way.

In both the main training room and the small antechamber, where men and women less worthy of adoration attempted to chisel away unwanted pounds and excess flesh, Sandefur was king. He had the ability to turn even the softest mass of human flesh into a hardened block of marble with the qualities of Michelangelo's David.

Since Cat survived a brutal attack by the Ribbon Rapist in 2006, she and Marci had upped their skills in self-defense. Both were experts in Krav Maga, the official hand-to-hand combat system used by Israeli Defense Forces. Krav Maga's use of quick counterattacks and searing offensive techniques made it the ideal fighting style for dangerous and unexpected situations. It was the preferred method of self-defense for the U.S. military and law enforcement personnel across the country.

As the sun attempted to crack the distant horizon, Cat and Marci were unaware that they would be putting their mental acuity skills to practical use later in the day -- just hours after that same sun had once again surrendered to the night. Had someone told them that Sandefur's secret extra-curricular activities would be the focus of their investigation, they would have laughed themselves silly.

**TOTAL SUBMISSION**
**COMING IN 2019**

# THROUGH THICK AND THIN

## THE FIRST CAT LEIGH AND MARCI WELLES CRIME NOVEL

## PROLOGUE

*O*ctober 2006

"I hate death. I especially hate the people who make death their life's work."

Cat Leigh, 30, but looking like a fresh-faced college cheerleader, sat on her living room sofa muttering while sifting through a stack of 8x10 glossies. Her long blonde hair hung down around her face like a curtain, hiding the piercing blue eyes that stared hard at the images of death before her. If appearances are deceiving, then Cat was the ultimate chameleon. Dressed in navy blue Capri pants, navy and white stripped short-sleeve cotton sweater and red low-heeled sandals, she appeared ready for a day of boating not one spent examining corpses and interviewing murder suspects.

One by one she held a magnifying glass to the photos and looked for something—anything—that would put an end to the reign of terror that had taken hold in Palm Beach County and, in particular, her hometown of Palm Beach Gardens, Florida and the neighboring town of Jupiter. Larger and more heavily populated West Palm Beach, a city to the south, was also caught in the grip of this diabolical crime spree.

The Kalendar Killer, christened by a local reporter with degrees in both English Literature and Theology, had left his victims displayed like gifts wrapped in banners celebrating the holiday of the month. The reporter, not content to merely slap the madman with a media worthy nickname, chose to use the ecclesiastic spelling... a not-so-subtle message that God had been missing in action when the crimes were committed.

So far, there had been five murders: Janice Handera, 47, married, stabbed through the throat with a nine-inch steel florist's pick on Mother's Day; Wallace Lanier, 60, a deadbeat dad, buried up to his neck and "stoned" to death with baseballs on Father's Day; PFC Timothy Varde, 23, bayoneted on July 4th; Peter Colangelo, 63, retired president of the local Electrical Workers Union, hung with a heavy duty extension cord from a Gumbo Limbo tree on Labor Day; and Amber Culp, 28, a palm reader with one of the smaller traveling circuses that made their way up and down the east coast, suffocated with tarot cards shoved down her throat on Halloween.

No connections had been found between the victims, no usable evidence was uncovered at the scenes and other than Lanier's history of non-support for his three children, the victims appeared to be decent people. The holiday banners in which the victims were wrapped were a dime a dozen in every party store in the country and on the internet. None of the local stores had surveillance video and, since hundreds of people had bought the banners... well, to quote one store owner, "You think I can remember every person who bought decorations over the past year. Think again!" If there was anything to be thankful for, it was that no murders occurred in August—a month with no recognized holidays.

Located at the north end of Palm Beach County, Palm Beach Gardens and Jupiter, the formerly quaint fishing villages on growth hormones, had zip codes that were popular winter destinations for wealthy retirees who called the northeast home only during the spring and summer. Come November, thousands of snowbirds, as they were less than affectionately called by the locals, arranged for their BMWs and Mercedes to be shipped to their temporary residences in the

Sunshine State via auto transport. They booked first class tickets on not-so-first-class airlines and flew south before a single flake of white marred their manicured lawns; firm believers that it was better to sweat than to shiver.

For those fanatics who carried a golf club bag like a dowager's hump, Palm Beach Gardens was heaven on earth. There were 12 USGA rated courses within the city limits and the

Professional Golfers Association of America was headquartered on the Avenue of Champions inside PGA National Resort and Spa, one of two sites which annually hosted the Honda Classic; the other being the Country Club at Mirasol.

Both Palm Beach Gardens and Jupiter were home to some very famous people in show business and the sports world, and Jupiter also had the distinction of being rated the Ninth Happiest Seaside Town in America by Coastal Living. With the potential for more murders hanging heavy in the air, there were no waits to tee off, the driving ranges and putting greens were empty, and the smiles of North County residents had turned into grimaces of fear.

Even the citizens of West Palm Beach, for whom the sound of sirens was a nightly occurrence, were behaving less apathetically than usual. Many were spending their evenings at home, which was putting a crimp in revenues at popular nightclubs and bars on trendy Clematis Street and at restaurants in upscale City Place. With each murder, the economy was becoming as big a concern for local government as crime statistics.

Headlines on the front page of the Palm Beach Post, the forever shrinking newspaper which was little more than a directory of new and used automobiles for sale, fairly shouted demands for answers. In every edition, the mayors and councils of every city in the county were quoted hurling verbal assaults on Sheriff Mike Brickshaw and some were threatening to drop the Palm Beach County Sheriff's Office from their payrolls.

Brickshaw's constant assurances that PBSO homicide detectives were working overtime to discover the identity of the Kalendar Killer had done little to assuage their concerns. The Sheriff himself had been issuing a few threats, telling his staff if he heard any of them using the made-for-tv sobriquet he would fire them.

Among local law enforcement and across the country, a deep dislike for crime shows such as the popular Las Vegas based CSI had been intensifying over the past few years. The public's belief that the technology seen on these shows actually existed had put an added burden on already overworked staff to solve crimes quickly.

Although the FBI's Integrated Automated Fingerprint Identification System could provide results in as little as 27 minutes, DNA processing could take weeks to months and sometimes years. When you considered that an estimated 400,000 rape kits were waiting to be processed nationwide, crime solving took on a whole new perspective.

Sheriff Brickshaw was often heard to state in his *I dare you to contradict me* voice, "Wouldn't it be wonderful if crimes could be solved in the time between commercials for urinary incontinence and erectile dysfunction."

Unselfconsciously, Cat spoke aloud to Kneesaa, the little black and white Shih Tzu perched beside her. Despite the dog's powder puff appearance, she was more protective of Cat than any ten-times-her-size Rottweiler and, judging by the attentive look in her eyes, Kneesaa understood every word her mistress was saying.

"We need a miracle, NeeNee," Cat whispered to Kneesaa, using her nickname for the dog. "What if we don't find this guy before Thanksgiving?"

The simple act of communication seemed to have a calming effect on Cat, who cradled the dog in her arms and buried her face in the scruff of her neck. A few seconds later, the dog squirmed away and Cat once again began to scowl. She returned to looking at the photos, frustration obvious in the Frisbee-like way she tossed each one to the floor.

The carpeting around Cat's feet was littered with throw aways— those pictures that documented the depravity of mankind while providing nothing new in the way of hope. Newspapers from weeks past, highlighted in yellow and circled in black, were stacked on the cushion next to her. So intent was she on looking for clues that the banging of the apartment complex maintenance man installing a new air conditioner in the kitchen was like a cotton ball bouncing on concrete.

So many people had tried to fix the rusting parts that Cat had grown immune to the sound of wrenches and saws hacking away at the old plumbing running through the walls of her second floor unit. Weekly complaints over the last three months had finally gotten her the result she wanted—a new a/c with the power to keep her apartment and her temper cool even on the hottest of days.

Only the ringing of the maintenance man's cell phone, which played an offensive rap tune with each incoming call, got Cat's attention. With irritation, she mumbled aloud, "Why that song?"

The droning sounds of the morning news anchors coming from the television were mere white noise until the voice of one of Cat's favorite "shiny girls" broke through her concentration. Shiny girls— that was what Cat called the overly sunny personalities of the local female weather forecasters who were more annoying than informative. Usually, this was the point at which she turned off the news, but on this morning Cat reached for the remote and amped up the volume as the map of south Florida filled the screen.

"For a few days, our normally cool October weather will be replaced with the sweltering heat of summer so dress accordingly," bubbled the early morning Miss Shiny, who was clad in a too tight, low cut dress left over from some long forgotten holiday party.

"Wardrobe advice from a wannabe actress. I guess she doesn't own a mirror, NeeNee. That outfit is better suited to New Year's Eve at a strip club than morning television."

Cat picked up Kneesaa's rubber chew toy from the floor and threw it at the widescreen across the room. She shook her head in wry amazement and reached again for Kneesaa. "Well,

NeeNee, shall we take bets on how Marci will be dressed today?"

The look in Kneesaa's eyes seemed to say, "You have to ask?"

Cat clicked off the television and returned to looking at the photographs, effectively blocking out the world around her. Deeply engrossed, she failed to hear the maintenance man announce his pending departure.

"Miss."

The tall, muscular black man in his early twenties adjusted the Bluetooth in his ear and pulled the brim of his baseball cap low on his face as he called to Cat from the hallway between the kitchen and living room. When she did not answer, he raised his voice slightly and tried again. "Miss, I'm leaving. If you have any more problems, please call the office."

Again Cat didn't acknowledge his presence and, again, he raised his voice. Kneesaa growled in response to its aggressive tone. Cat looked at NeeNee, who was staring into the hallway. Following the dog's gaze, she saw but didn't make eye contact with the repairman as she offered a response. His back was now towards her as he prepared to exit the apartment. "Did you say something?"

The maintenance man spoke over his shoulder. "I'm leaving. If you have any problems, call the office."

Cat, who had already turned back to studying the crime scene photos, waved a hand in acknowledgment as the maintenance man opened the front door. "Thanks."

The next thing Cat heard was a scream, which barely caused her to flinch.

"Yikes!" Cat's partner, Marci Welles, yelped as she stood in the doorway, blocking the maintenance man's exit.

Cat looked at Kneesaa and rolled her eyes. With photographs still in hand, she called to her dearest friend to enter. "Nice of you to wake the neighborhood, Marci. Come on in."

Short and pleasingly plump Marci was dressed in a man-tailored, long-sleeve shirt, suit jacket and heavy rubber soled tie shoes. Her boyish haircut was softened by long bangs which framed mischievous dark eyes and a pert little nose. Freckles were scattered over her cheeks like soot that had drifted on the wind. Her raspy voice held a tinge of suppressed laughter. "You scared the crap out of me," Marci joked with the repairman who, with head lowered, side stepped around her. Mumbling, "Sorry," he moved quickly down the stairs. "No problem. Now, at least, I have an excuse for the gray streaks in my hair."

The maintenance man didn't respond. Marci shrugged her shoulders at his rudeness and moved into the apartment, closing the door behind her.

"Are you ready?" Marci called to Cat as she strode into the living room. "They're waiting for us."

"Yeah, I'm just going over the shots from the Blowing Rocks murder."

Marci threw a manila envelope onto the coffee table. "Here. Look at these. I guarantee they won't make you cringe."

As Cat opened the envelope, Marci picked up Kneesaa and rubbed her belly. She directed her comments to the dog but the intended recipient was well within earshot. "NeeNee, your mommy needs to get a life."

Cat stuck her tongue out at Marci as she withdrew another stack of photos from the envelope. A huge smile crossed her face. "Oh, Marci, these are precious."

"Yup. Your goddaughter is one cute kid even if I do say so myself."

"You and Ian are so lucky."

"You'll have one of your own before long."

"Maybe."

"Definitely," Marci assured her with a punch to the shoulder. "But right now we've got a hot one waiting for us downtown." Marci gave Kneesaa a final rub on the belly and laid her back on the sofa.

Rising from the sofa, Cat gave Marci's outfit the once over. "Hot being the definitive word, Marci. You do know that it's 96 degrees outside, don't you?"

"Your point?"

"You're dressed for winter—in Vermont."

"I look professional."

"I'll remind you of that statement in an hour when you're struggling to breathe and dripping like a melting icicle." Cat turned and headed for the front door. Kneesaa followed her. "Sorry, sweet pea. No time for a walk now. Be a good girl while I'm gone."

In the small alcove off the entranceway, Cat opened the drawer of an antique credenza. She removed a holstered gun and a gold detective's shield on a lanyard. She took the gun from the holster, snapped in a clip and slid the gun back into the holster before dropping it into her satchel, which was hanging on a nearby coat rack. She slipped the lanyard around her neck and tucked the badge inside her shirt. Marci, anxious to get on the road, already had her hand on the door. Cat stopped her as she was about to step onto the porch.

"Are you sure you don't want to change into something cooler?"

"I'm fine. This is my signature look."

"Whatever you say, Nanook. Lead the way."

# CHAPTER ONE

$S$eptember 2007

Detective Marcassy Welles—Marci to her friends, and Detective Jessica Leigh— affectionately called Cat—had been a big part of each other's lives long before they became partners in the Homicide Division of the Palm Beach County Sheriff's Office. Best friends since freshman year at Wellington High School, the differences in their physical appearance were often fodder for jokes cruel and kind perpetrated by their classmates. From the beginning, they had watched each other's backs at all times. Pity the poor fool who tried to hurt either one of them be it with a gun, a knife or sweet words that broke a trusting heart.

Known for being quick on the comeback, brunette Marci was round and short—4'11" but adamant that she was five feet tall. Her turned-up nose and laughing hazel eyes gave her an impish appearance, which many a criminal had learned had nothing to do with her unswerving dedication to upholding the law. Her relentless pursuit of those who didn't share her penchant for order and justice was legendary.

The more serious Cat was a statuesque 5'10" with nearly waist length blonde hair and big blue oval-shaped eyes. Those eyes were the reason for the nickname her Aunt Annie had bestowed upon her when just a toddler. "Jessicat" had been shortened to "Cat" as the lithe little girl grew into a lovely young woman.

Cat, like Marci, saw the world in black and white. What was wrong was wrong and what was right was right. There was no gray area where excuses justified hurting another human being except in self-defense. Both women were resolute in their pursuit of those who thumbed their noses at the justice system, rarely finding a reason to cut an offender any slack.

Eighteen months earlier, Marci, 31, and her husband, Ian, had adopted a beautiful baby girl, Sonora Leslie. Having waited a long time for the fulfillment of this dream, their lives were now complete.

Cat, whose beauty had intimidated many men, was finally in a serious relationship that appeared to be heading for the marriage aisle. Having recently crossed into the third decade of her life, she had struggled to find Mr. Right and feared that her sudden good fortune was just a nasty bit of teasing on the part of fate. The two couples spent most of their downtime together and had forged a bond that was titanium strong.

In spite of all the ugliness the women saw daily, they had refused to let disillusion creep into their souls and change their naturally kind and caring personalities. Although they strove to always see the good in people, they were not averse to drawing their guns and using them when necessary. Both were thankful that so far in their careers they had not had to shoot to kill but knowing the possibility existed, their marksmanship skills were exemplary.

Cat and Marci were different from most of the people in their social circle in that their self-esteem was not raised by frequenting the latest hot spots which sucked a wallet dry with hype and hand stamps. They preferred beer and burgers over the fancy meals served at popular City Place haunts and at restaurants on Snob Island—their name for Palm Beach.

Eight years earlier, they had joined the Palm Beach County Sheriff's Office and, after four years on the streets, had been promoted to detectives in the Homicide Division. In the early years, Marci and Cat often worked separately, but their Sergeant soon realized that, while alone they were formidable, together they were an unstoppable force.

The majority of their peers respected them for their ethics and for working their butts off to put criminals behind bars. There were a few, however, who felt diminished by successful women in the male-dominated profession of law enforcement. Those men assuaged their egos by referring to Marci and Cat as "Thick" and "Thin," a reference to the women's appearance that said more about the men than the women they were describing. Cat and Marci referred to them collectively as "the assholes."

On this Labor Day morning, the sky was glazed with golden hues when Marci and Cat pulled into the lot at Coral Cove Park on Jupiter Island. The sand blowing in from the beach covered the macadam, obscuring the white lines that marked off the parking spaces. Not that finding an actual parking space would have been possible. Between the six Jupiter PD vehicles, two ambulances and what appeared to be at least 40 privately-owned automobiles, the place resembled Sound Advice Amphitheater in the aftermath of a heavy metal concert.

Marci brought the late model Ford Crown Victoria to a stop on the grass that cushioned the children's playground. She and Cat sat quietly, mentally preparing themselves for another day of murder and mayhem. In the glow of the newly awakened dawn, four swings moved rhythmically to and fro, as though ghostly sprites were watching them, witnesses to what had been and what was yet to be.

Marci stared out the windshield as she ruminated aloud. "Two things I really hate—September and this."

"This what?"

With a nod of her head, Marci indicated the swings while nibbling a hangnail on her index finger. "This… the playground so close to a death. Just doesn't seem right."

"That's the new mommy in you talking. Before Sonora was born, you never noticed the grisly stuff."

Marci's response was muffled as she continued to chew on her hangnail.

"I can't understand you if you talk with your fingers in your mouth. Who's the baby—you or Sonora?"

"I was just thinking." Marci removed a wet index finger from her mouth and pointed it at Cat. "Do you remember last Labor Day? We spent it at Blowing Rocks investigating one of the Kalendar Killer murders."

"Peter Colangelo. His memory did cross my mind. Let's hope whatever we find here isn't as gruesome."

"I think of those five people a lot. Probably, too often."

"Me, too. That was a tough seven months. Tough for us. Tougher for the families of the victims."

Marci answered by crossing her middle finger over the still wet index finger and holding them up for Cat to see. "Are you sure you're ready to go back to work?"

"Don't let the black eyes and bandages fool you. I was ready seven weeks ago when you kicked me out of the office and told me I had to rest."

"Did you?"

"Rest?"

"I know. Stupid question." Marci resumed nibbling while staring at the swings a few minutes longer.

**Seven weeks earlier:**

When Marci arrived at police headquarters, she found her partner sitting at her desk staring at a computer screen. Just two days after a brutal attack, Cat's appearance was shocking. Her long hair was pulled back into a pony tail revealing a badly bruised and disfigured face. Her lips and nose were swollen; her eyes were black. There was a large bandage around her neck; blood oozing slowly through the gauze. Cat's left shoulder was immobilized in a sling.

"What the hell are you doing here?"

"I'm fine... other than looking like the Elephant Man."

"You are not fine, Cat. You need rest. It's only been two days."

"I said I'm fine."

"You're supposed to talk to the department shrink before you can be cleared for duty."

"I cleared myself. What evidence do you have so far? Did you talk to the women in the management office?"

"I really do wish you would go home." Marci pleaded with Cat only to be ignored. "Okay. Have it your way. Nothing. We've learned nothing. The office manager claimed they don't have a maintenance man who resembles your attacker. She has no idea who he was."

"How could that be? How would he know my a/c wasn't working if not through the management office?"

"She's lying. She's trying to protect their corporate ass."

Cat sat quietly, deep in thought. Officers and clerical staff walked by, shooting veiled glances in her direction. Some proffered sympathetic smiles. She scowled back at them. A cadet brought a cup of coffee, put it on the desk without saying a word and hurried away. Cat mumbled her thanks and sipped carefully from the cup; the pain from the deep cuts inside her mouth sending shivers across her shoulders as the hot coffee flowed over them.

"Please go home and get some rest."

"We have other cases. Death doesn't take a vacation because a police officer gets attacked. You work the active ones. I'll work mine."

"You're too close to this."

"I'll do desk duty. You do the field work. I need this, Marci. I need to stay busy."

"Okay. I'm sure you've gone through the mug shots. Anything?"

"No. There's no one in our data base who resembles that bastard."

"You're sure."

"His face is seared into my brain, Marci. I'm sure."

"Once the DNA sample is processed, we can run it through CODIS."

"Unless I'm his first…"

"Then, let's make you his last. Now, go home."

~

Marci shook off the remainder of her reverie and returned to the present. She exhaled a deep sigh and reached for the door handle. As the lock clicked open, she turned to Cat. "You can't pretend the attack didn't happen. You almost died. That's not something you can ignore."

"I'm not ignoring it, Marci. I'm just not letting it rule my life. I'm fine."

Marci nodded her understanding, a finger stuck between her teeth. She gave the door a push with her foot. It swung open and back, crushing her leg and forcing her to bite down hard on her finger. "Shit!"

"When are you going to learn not to do that?"

"Kick the door?"

"Yes, and chew at your hangnails. Get a manicure."

"I'm never getting another manicure." Marci threw a look at Cat that needed no explanation.

"You're ridiculous."

"But irresistible." Marci continued to suck on her finger as though it was a lollipop. "That hurt."

"I'm surprised you have any feeling left in your fingers. Actually, I'm surprised you have any fingers at all the way you bite them."

"I still have the ability to raise one in a single digit salute."

Marci made a fist in front of Cat's face and slowly began to lift her middle finger. Cat playfully smacked Marci's hand out of the way.

"If it wasn't for me always nagging you," Cat defended her behavior, "you'd have ten bloody stumps by now, and you'd be wearing your wedding ring through your nose."

"I know you're talking. I can see your lips moving, but I don't hear a sound. Let's go to work. Neither the law nor the dead like to be kept waiting."

"In my experience, waiting is all the dead will be doing for the rest of eternity so a few more minutes won't matter," Cat informed her while reaching across the seat and pulling Marci's hand out of her mouth. "Don't be so stubborn. If you keep doing that, you're going to get an infection."

"Been doing it since high school—ever since I found out that chubby girls don't make the cheerleading squad."

"You tried out just to annoy Tammy Burns. You never wanted to be a cheerleader."

"I hated Tammy Burns and…" Marci bit skin from her finger, "… my feelings were hurt."

"They were not! You enjoyed every moment she suffered watching you mangle the cheers. Please! Stop biting your finger."

Marci picked the piece of skin from her tongue and flicked it into the air. Cat gagged, "That's disgusting!"

"I hate it when you're preachy."

"You hate it when I'm right."

"That, too."

Through the rearview mirror, Marci saw the coroner's car and van vying for a spot. The last to arrive, the medical examiner and his assistants were forced to park at the curb, half in and half out of the park entrance. "G's here."

"Thanks for the warning."

Marci tossed the car keys to Cat with her usual request, "Hold on to these for me, will ya? I don't have any pockets. And… be nice to G."

Cat grabbed her satchel from the floor and dropped the keys into it as Marci gave the door another shove; this time putting out her hand to stop it from wreaking further damage to her leg. One foot emerged from the driver's side wearing sensible rubber soled shoes with laces neatly tied in a bow.

Dressed in her usual dark pants, man-tailored shirt and blazer, Marci stood beside the car and removed a crumbled tissue from the sleeve of her jacket. On the front of her shirt, the beginnings of a wet spot could be seen where her bra met her rib cage. She pushed her already damp bangs out of her eyes and held them in place with a bobbie pin she retrieved from the car's no longer used ash tray. Wiping the tissue over her face, she lamented to Cat, "I hate September!"

"You already said that."

From the passenger side of the car, another foot emerged. Polished toes peeked out from low-heeled sling back pumps. Cat was dressed in light weight casual clothing and appeared perspiration free. Carefully applied makeup artfully concealed the remains of two black eyes, leaving what appeared to be dark circles from lack of sleep—a plausible explanation accepted by anyone familiar with Cat's dedication to her job. A surgical dressing wrapped around her throat was partially hidden by the collar of her shirt. Despite the bandage's wide width, the raw edges of a deep cut could be seen along the left side of Cat's neck.

Marci walked around the car and looked at Cat's feet with feigned annoyance. "You can't wear those shoes on the beach. Did you remember to bring something appropriate?"

"Appropriate? Like what? Combat boots?"

Cat indicated Marci's shoes with a nod of her head. She reached into her satchel and pulled out a pair of leather thongs. With a practiced step, she tossed her shoes into the car and slipped quickly into the sandals. "Don't worry. I've got my Dolce Vitas right here."

Marci rolled her eyes at Cat as she licked away the sweat dripping from her upper lip. "The model with the magnum—you kill me."

"Don't even say that in jest."

Her face showing instant regret, Marci apologized. "I'm sorry, Cat. You're so damned determined not to let the attack change you that sometimes I forget just how close you came to not being here."

"He got three and a half hours, Marci. He's not getting another minute. Can we go to work now?"

With the wind moaning softly over the dunes and through the palmettos, the two detectives walked side by side toward the bright ball of fire that ruled over the distant waves and the nearby shores. The sun was up, and its power was not to be denied.

"Damn, it's a frickin' scorcher!" Marci again wiped her face with the tissue hidden in the sleeve of her jacket.

"And going to get hotter but we've had this conversation many times over the years. If you weren't so thick headed…"

"I'm not thick headed. I'm professional."

"You're also a sweaty mess and, eventually, you'll be 'tinky.'" Cat waved her hand in front of her nose, mimicking Marci's 18-month-old daughter. Her voice accurately captured one of the few phrases the little girl could say.

Marci's laugh echoed across the parking lot as she dipped her head to her armpit, sniffed, and then spun around so that she was walking backward. She lifted her arm and offered Cat a whiff. "Spring time fresh. Smell for yourself."

"No, thanks. Besides, I said 'eventually.' Springtime fresh will become summer stench in a few hours. Trust me."

Cat pulled her sunglasses from her pocket and slipped them over her squinting eyes. "Did you remember to bring your Foster Grants, Ms. Professional?"

Before Marci could answer, Doctor Mark Geschwer, the much respected medical examiner who was called "G" by everyone, hailed them from the parking lot in his best Jerry Lewis impersonation. "Detective Ladies! Yoo hoo! Detective Ladies."

"Pretend you don't hear him." Cat, visibly cringing, urged Marci to keep walking.

"He's harmless."

A huge fan of the well-known comedian, G's imitations left much to be desired, but his attempts to mimic the king of clowns usually elicited laughs from department personnel. He was fond of saying that it was better to do a lousy impersonation of a comic than a great imper-sonation of a corpse.

"He drives me crazy." Cat hastened her steps. "I just don't get his fascination with Jerry Lewis. Jerry Lewis! Why can't he admire Richard Pryor?"

"Pryor's dead."

"Yeah, I know, and if G continues speaking in that annoying voice, I might set him on fire."

"Remind me not to piss you off."

G's voice called out to Marci and Cat again, still imitating Jerry Lewis.

"Walk faster," Cat urged, giving Marci a shove.

# ABOUT THE AUTHOR

**Donna M. Carbone** is an author and playwright. For five years, her unfiltered opinion column appeared in *The Beacon Magazine*. She is a frequent contributor to the *Jupiter Courier Magazine*. Donna is the author of the Cat Leigh and Marci Welles crime novels set in Palm Beach County. *Through Thick and Thin* and *Silk Suit/Stone Heart* use the true account of her daughter's kidnapping and rape in 2007 to focus a spotlight on crimes against women. The third book, *Total Submission*, is currently being written. She is also the author of *Private Hell,* which focuses on domestic abuse, a semi-autobiographical crime novel. Her first children's book, *Lambie and Me*, is based on conversations with her grandson, Blake.

Donna's play, *Shell of a Man*, was presented at the Dallas Convention Center and the Burt Reynolds Institute for Film and Theatre. Her one-man show, *Fear Sells,* was presented at the TEDxJupiter conference in 2013.

Donna is an outspoken advocate for victims of violent crimes and better healthcare for our veterans. She is a huge supporter of literacy and promotes indie authors in Palm Beach and Martin Counties through her *A Novel Approach to Literacy* author meet and greet events.

Her most recent book, (co-authored with Rosario Liotta) *Bread and Bullets - The Rosario Liotta Story* - is a true crime novel and an insider's look at crime and the criminal justice system.

You can learn more about Donna on her website: writeforyoullc.com

Made in the USA
Columbia, SC
26 November 2023

26710115R00113